The savvy cheer squad at Gro...
Their routines are ...
going to win. Co...
fresh guys playir ...
many prima don ...
being dynamic ar ...
....

VICTORIA

SAVVY
Girl

Victoria House has all kinds of hang-ups.
She's shy. She's gullible. She's vulnerable.
A perfect target for mean girls.

ALL
IN

Stephanie Perry Moore

SAVVY GIRL

Forever Hot

Golden Heart

Scream Loud

All In

Real Diva

Copyright © 2014 by Saddleback Educational Publishing

ISBN-13: 978-1-62250-686-6
ISBN-10: 1-62250-686-3
eBook: 978-1-61247-751-0

Printed in Guangzhou, China
NOR/1113/CA21302124

18 17 16 15 14   1 2 3 4 5

To Lois Barney, Perlicia Floyd & Persephanie Sims
(My cheer mom girlfriends)

Having girlfriends is something I treasure. We laugh, we share things, and we have each other's backs. We help each other make sure the cheerleaders are on point.

Keep on giving everything to help the girls stay great. The way you care blesses so many. May every reader be as great a friend as you all are.

Know I'm thankful you're in my life. I love you!

ACKNOWLEDGEMENTS

It is understandable to want to look and feel beautiful. You want your friends to think you're cute. You don't want your appearance to be criticized by your parents. You want to look in the mirror and feel satisfied. However, the pressures in life can make you feel like you don't measure up. You may get desperate to make changes and make unhealthy choices.

I enjoyed telling this story because though you may feel overwhelmed, life is precious and worth living. Tomorrow is not promised, so every day needs to be filled with gladness. If you want to work on you, go all in and do it the right way. Hurting yourself or getting down on yourself is not productive. You can be the best you if you want to be. Real talk ... don't take shortcuts, don't try to do it all alone, and don't let anyone hold you back.

Here is a considerable thank you to everyone who helps me stay all in with my novels.

Acknowledgements

For my parents, Dr. Franklin and Shirley Perry, thanks for instilling in me that I am fine just the way God made me. I am all in every aspect of my life.

For my publisher, especially the designer, Ashley Thompson, thanks to your belief in my writing, I am able to be all in with this fun series.

For my extended family: brother, Dennis Perry, mother-in-law, Ann Redding, godmother, Marjorie Kimbrough, and goddaughter, Danielle Lynn, thanks for your continued support that keeps me feeling good about me. I am all in when I speak to young people because I always want them to feel great about themselves.

For my assistants: Candace Johnson, Shaneen Clay, and Alyxandra Pinkston, thanks to your help, I can be all in with the writing and make deadlines.

For my friends who are dear to my heart: Gwen Tatum, Leslie Perry, Sarah Lundy, Jenell Clark, Nicole Smith, Jackie Dixon, Kim Forest, Vickie Davis, Kim Monroe, Jamell Meeks, Dayna Fleming, Michele Jenkins, Megan Ray, Kim Garner, Lakeba Williams, Veronica Evans, Laurie Weaver, Yolanda Rodgers-Howsie, and Denise Gilmore, thanks to your friendship I am all in with making the characters have real friendships, because I know first-hand what that feels like.

For my teens: Dustyn, Sydni, and Sheldyn, thanks to your fun lives of being a football player and cheerleaders, you help me be all in with accuracy.

For my husband, Derrick, thanks to your love I can be all in and write stories that warm the soul.

For my new readers, thanks to you for checking out my work. I am all in giving everything I've got to each word in hopes that you enjoy it.

And my Savior, thanks to your plan for my life, I'm happily and thankfully all in, using the pen to prayerfully make a difference.

CHAPTER ONE

Gathering Evidence

I'm a big, fat pig. I'm a big, fat pig, and I know it. I know it," I said to myself because all I could think about was food.

We had just won a big football game. Everybody was ecstatic on the field, and I was thinking about where I was going to go to eat. I was actually happy the game was over, not because it was a nail-biter or because my half-sister Vanessa's new boo, Emerson Prince, won the game with his kick, but because I had been holding my stomach in all game, and now I could let it out a little. Okay, I was letting it out a lot. Problem was, when I did that, my tan-colored gut bulged out. At least I thought so. I really needed to find a safety pin because when Emerson's kick made it through the uprights, I did a herkie and popped the button on the back of my skirt. I had hoped the zipper would hold my skirt together, but as I walked around I could feel it sliding down. I knew I needed to get to my cheer bag to put on my jogging pants.

"Oh my gosh! We won the game!" Vanessa said with glee, running over to me.

She was jumping up and down. I wanted to be happy for her. I could only imagine all she'd been through—not living with her mom and younger half siblings because her mother couldn't take care of her, having to live with my family when she felt like an outsider because, though we shared the same dad, my father chose my mom over hers, and being hospitalized. She'd been so depressed that she made some bad choices that had almost ended her life.

I was jealous of all the attention she was getting from our folks, but she and I talked about it. We had a fresh start, and I didn't want to ruin it by not being happy for her. However, I couldn't jump up and down with her because I might lose my drawers.

"What's wrong? I know you, girl. You're not excited," Vanessa said, clearly salty, until she looked at the game's star. "Is he not just the most handsome thing?"

Admittedly, Emerson was a cutie pie. She'd never known it, but I had a bad crush on him in the eighth grade. I thought we were perfect for each other. Both of us were mixed, Caucasian and African American. I wanted a good boy, and he was a good boy—the son of a preacher man.

When we got to high school, the crush melted like ice left out in the sun. Emerson wasn't as cool anymore. He wasn't hanging with the right crowd. I guess I was shallow, all into image and status, and Emerson didn't have those things. Well, until now. I didn't want him again or anything. I'd actually taken the initiative and told him he needed to make sure he didn't lose Vanessa. Everyone in the school knew he wanted her, but when she finally gave him the time of day, he started tripping. But come to find out, he was the target of a gang, so he deserved a pass for being preoccupied. It was actually admirable that he'd kept his distance from her so that Vanessa wouldn't get mixed up in the violence while the gang was trying to hurt him.

"I'm fine. I'm okay. Go enjoy him." I pushed her toward Emerson.

"Okay, okay. I just can't believe he won the game! He was the kicker! Isn't that crazy?"

"Yes, that's crazy. And he likes you."

She squeezed me real tight.

There were so many of us on the field. Everyone was slapping each other's hands. I got caught up in the emotions, and before I knew it, I was being twirled in the air.

"We won!" Stone Bush, the fine, perfectly tanned, sandy-brown-haired stud, said.

I didn't know it would feel so good to have his strong arms around me. But as heavy as I thought I was, he made me feel light and special. Stone was a hunk. He'd always been tall and lanky, but now he was filled out too. Word was that he was one of the best tight ends in the state. Since he was just a junior, colleges were hitting him hard, loving his almost six-foot-three, 230-pound frame. Of course I thought he was handsome with his slick hair. He was cool like his dad, who was a rock star in one of the hottest bands in the land.

However, he said, "Dang, you're more solid than you look."

Then something inside me snapped, and I said, "I didn't ask you to pick me up!"

"I was just teasing," he said, looking worried that he'd offended me.

Not falling for his pitiful expression, I said, "Whatever."

"Yeah, glad you know he's not teasing," said Jillian Grayson, a brash competition cheerleader who got on my nerves.

She was such a dream killer. She had a boy-friend, but he moved away. Now it was like she wanted every guy in our school to like her, even the ones who were already taken.

She leaned in and whispered, "You need to go fix your clothes. You're about to lose your skirt."

Horrified, I was standing there in the middle of the field surrounded by people. Where could I turn? Where could I go? How could I get away from everyone? I stood there frozen, looking at Stone, who was laughing. He was talking to some of his other teammates, so he probably wasn't laughing at me, but I felt like he was anyway.

"You need to go fix your clothes. Didn't you hear me?" Jillian said, even more loudly this time.

"Shhh!" I said, looking at her unbelievingly. "I don't want everybody in the world to know!"

Frowning at me like I stunk, Jillian uttered, "You're getting too fat. You can't order a small-sized uniform at the beginning of the year and need an extra-large before the season is out."

"I am not that big."

She rolled her eyes, insinuating otherwise. "I've been noticing you at practice and stuff. You've always got something in your mouth. No need to look at guys like Stone."

I wanted to tell her she was lying. I wanted to go off on her and say it was none of her business. But the only thing I could do was look at her tiny little waist and say, "How do you stay so thin?"

With a smirk she bragged, "I eat everything I want."

Rolling my eyes, I knew what worked for her could not work for me. "Okay, well, not all of us can do that."

She leaned in closer. "You can if you do what I do. I purge."

I didn't understand what she meant. Then she took her finger and pointed it down her throat. I felt my eyes widen as I realized she meant she threw up her food. She hushed me before I could overreact.

"Your skirt looks hideous because your zipper is way down. I'll just follow you to the bathroom so you can change."

"I got to go to the sidelines and get my bag."

"Okay, I'll follow you over there."

"You'll stay close to me?" I asked.

"Sure," she said.

I couldn't believe Jillian was being so nice. I should've known something was up. We hadn't gone two feet before we bumped into Stone. Jillian moved away, leaving my problem exposed. Stone was standing directly behind me. I quickly turned.

"Your skirt," he said, truly rattling me.

I just grabbed the back of it and ran over to the fence. How could Jillian do that to me? Why would she allow me to be embarrassed?

I pulled up my pants under my skirt,

then slid the skirt over them to take it off. As I was changing, I looked back over and saw her flirting with Stone. No wonder she wanted to make me look like an idiot. She wanted him all to herself. And why would I think he wanted me when she was so much hotter and white? I'd never known Stone to claim a girlfriend, but of all the girls I'd seen him with, none had my makeup.

In addition to my skin color, I was a big, fat pig, and I knew it. Now that I knew something I could do about it, what was I going to do? I knew I couldn't keep doing the same things because I wanted different results. I had to lose a few pounds in my gut. I was desperate, and I wasn't opposed to taking drastic measures, particularly if they could help.

"I got to go talk to my mom and dad!" Vanessa said, happier than I'd ever seen her, almost an hour after the game. "But I need you to see if you can get your mom's car because I'd like you to go out with me tonight so I can hang out with Emerson."

"He drives," I said, wanting her to get that

she couldn't just use me to accomplish her agenda.

"I know he drives, but I want to hang out with you. A bunch of us are going to meet up over there."

"Over where?" I asked real tired, hungry, and sort of irritated.

"I don't know. A couple of them were saying we should go to Chuck E. Cheese's. It's innocent fun that I want to share with my sister. Is that all right?" Vanessa said in a baby-talk voice.

Being real sisters was something I was going to have to get used to. I wanted to be left to myself because I felt so un-cute. But Chuck E. Cheese's meant pizza, and that hooked me. I was in.

I went up to my mom and said, "Vanessa and I want to hang out. Can I get the car? Can you ride back to the house with Dad after you guys drop off Vanessa's mom and siblings at the hotel?"

Smiling at the fact that I wanted to bond with Vanessa, she replied, "Yeah, I can ride with him. Sure."

"You sure you won't be too squeezed in the

Infiniti with Vanessa's mom, her three siblings, Junior, you, and Dad?"

"We'll work it out. You girls go and enjoy yourself." She leaned in and said, "I wish I had a sister."

I didn't know how to respond to that. For so long, Vanessa had been a thorn in my side, and while she said she felt bad for all that, she'd still ruined my life these past couple of years, always making me feel bad that I was the one who had my parents together. And now I was just supposed to forget all that? Nevertheless, I thanked my mom, and then Vanessa and I headed out.

"So we got to get you a boyfriend," my sister said, looking over at me as we drove to get something to eat. There was a caravan of folks behind us.

"I don't need a boyfriend. I'm cool by myself."

"I don't know who you think believes that, but I don't," my sister said.

"Well, it took you a long time to accept that Emerson was into you. Why can't you respect the fact that I don't need to be pushed either?"

"I'm not trying to push you. I can just see that you really want it. That's all."

"I don't know how you see that."

"Because I see you looking at Skylar and Ford, and I saw you on the field looking at me and Emerson. You can have that too." She paused, smacked her lips, and did a sister-girl move. "And I think I know who likes you."

I rolled my eyes, not wanting to know. I turned up the music, and she shook her head. At least the rest of the way we drove in peace.

When we got to Chuck E. Cheese's, Emerson immediately came over to my sister and placed his arm around her shoulder. To see her blush made me smile. I was happy she wasn't angry like she used to be. She and I had both been through a lot. She deserved some happiness.

When she sashayed off to the bathroom, Emerson came up to me and said, "Aight, I took your advice. Your sister and I are cool."

I grabbed his collar, twisted it, and said, "Just make sure you keep it that way."

After I let it go, he said, "I got you. I got you."

"Good job in the game by the way." I patted him on the back.

"Yeah, he did do a really good job, didn't he?"

Stone said, coming to stand beside me. I hadn't even seen him come into Chuck E. Cheese's.

Had I known he was going to be there, I probably wouldn't have come. Something about him was making my heart go pitter-patter, and that was the last thing I wanted from the last person I wanted. He was so sarcastic and such a jerk. I didn't want to like him only to be crushed, so I slid a couple of steps away from him.

"What? I got bad breath or something? Dang, every time I come around, you get all squirmy," Stone joked.

Boldly I retorted, "You wish."

"Emerson, wassup with her? Why won't she talk to me?" Stone asked playfully.

"Because you're not telling her you want to talk to her. What, you want her to make the first move or something?" Emerson asked him point blank.

Stone flushed and mumbled, "I just want us to be friends."

Emerson gave a sly giggle. "Oh, okay. Just friends. Right."

"What? What?" Stone said defensively. I knew he wasn't interested in more with me, so Emerson didn't need to make a big deal out of it.

The whole crew started piling in. Skylar and Ford, Yaris and Hagen, and Ariel and Ryder, though they were on-again, off-again.

Just as I was about to be thankful that Jillian was nowhere around, she stormed inside. With her hands on her hips, she shouted, "Why didn't you guys wait for me?"

"That should have been a clue we ain't wanting your tail around," Ryder yelled out. I liked the fact that he was so real and honest.

"I wasn't talking to you anyway, Ryder," Jillian told him.

Ryder had us all laughing when he mocked her whining tone and said, "Well, I *was* talking to you, Jillian."

"Can we just order?" I said as my stomach let out a little grumble.

"You would be the one ready to eat," Jillian said, trying to get a laugh. Instead everyone looked at her like, *You're crazy. Why would you say something like that?* She got defensive. "I'm just saying. The football players are the ones who played a tough game, and here's this cheerleader asking about food. Just seems a little odd."

"It's not odd," Vanessa said, coming out of the back area near the restrooms. I didn't even realize my sister was out of the bathroom, but she had my back. Vanessa continued, "They were playing a hard game, but we were yelling and screaming and jumping all over the place. I'm hungry too. You're the only anorexic up in here."

"I got your anorexic right here," Jillian said, stepping toward my sister.

I went over to Vanessa and said, "Thank you, sis, but she ain't worth it."

"You're certainly right about that," Vanessa said.

Jillian gave me a snide, "I'll-fix-you" type of grin. I smirked back at her. I was still mad at her tail for embarrassing me on the field.

After we all ordered, people started to pair off. Skylar and Ford were so cute, all snuggled up in a corner. Guys were trying to get him to play on some of the machines, but he didn't seem to want to leave her side. Vanessa and Emerson were playing, and Hagen and Yaris were arguing. Ryder was watching Ariel from the back. She knew it, and she was switching even harder.

"Our friends are funny, huh?" Stone came up behind me and said.

"You startled me."

"I'm sorry. I just wanted to see if you wanted to play a game or something. My treat," he said as he pulled out a token.

Thankfully, the pizza came out, and I didn't have to turn him down. Everyone was off doing his or her own thing, which was fine because I wanted to eat in peace. I was hungry and didn't want to try and be cute about it. I was hoping Stone wouldn't follow me to the table. But I didn't anticipate Jillian coming up beside him, taking him by the arm, and tugging him away.

"You said you wanted to play with me. Let's do it," Jillian said.

I looked away, and when I looked back, his hand was on her behind.

"Stop it!" Jillian was giggling like a girl being asked out for the first time.

He looked at her like she was crazy, but she came over to me, leaned in, and said, "No need to think about this one when you can see he wants me."

As I watched him wait for her to catch up with him and as I looked at everyone else with his or her boo, I realized maybe Vanessa was right. Maybe the facts were right there in front of me. I was a little antsy and a little hungry because I didn't like being alone. Before, alone had never been a bad thing. Now, though I didn't want to admit it to myself, there was a guy I was interested in, and I hated that he wasn't interested in me back.

"Did you have to eat all of the pizza?" I heard Ariel say in a smart-aleck way. I looked up and realized she was talking to me.

"I only ate three pieces. What are you talking about?"

"Five of us went in on the pizza. You were only supposed to have two slices. But I'm just kidding."

"Well, I let her have one of my slices!" my sister said, covering for me.

They were all looking at me like I was the greediest person they'd ever seen, or maybe I was just being paranoid. But the saddest part of all was that I was still hungry. What was happening to my body? Why was food on my mind all the time? My metabolism had changed.

"Somebody needs to give me a slice of pizza," Jillian said, even though she hadn't contributed any money toward it. When we all looked at her like she was nuts, she tried another route. "Aw, that's okay. I'll get it from Stone."

"Stone?" my sister asked, looking over at her like she didn't have a chance with him.

Jillian repeated, "Yes, I said Stone."

"Like he's interested in your stuck-up behind."

"Just as interested as Emerson is in your ugly one."

"Are you calling me ugly?"

"If you don't get your grades up, dummy, you might not be cheering."

"Wait, you're calling me a dummy too?" Vanessa asked.

"Just ignore her," I said.

Jillian said, "I'm just stating facts. Coach Pat put up the list of who's failing a class, and your sister's name was on it."

"There was no list put up, Jillian," Skylar corrected her.

Jillian quickly tried to cover her tracks. "You're right. He just gave a slip of paper to her tonight after the game, and if she pulls it out and reads it—"

"It's none of your business what it says."

"Well, he told us all that he was going to be doing that. We know what it says. You're the only one who got a letter. You're failing."

Another reason why my sister had been hostile toward me was because I was a better student than her. I never offered to help. Hearing that, it was very clear that my sister needed my help whether she wanted it or not. Her failing a class wasn't a possibility.

"Ugh, Skylar. You're going to have to do something about that horrible zit on your face," Jillian criticized, turning on her now.

"It is pretty big," Ariel laughed and said. "But I had one last week, so I'm not laughing."

"You are laughing," Skylar countered, appearing to be hurt by the fact that they were talking about her.

"Why are you reaching your hand over for my food?" Ariel said to Jillian.

Jillian bragged, " 'Cause, I can tell the guys

are sharing pizza. I know Stone would buy me one if I wanted, but ..."

Vanessa started coughing. I hit my sister in the arm. Vanessa didn't hold back. "She's so full of it. As if he really likes her."

"No, I've been watching. He does like her," I added under my breath.

Vanessa heard me and said, "Don't read too much into that. She's so manipulative." She turned to Jillian. "Don't you still go with ER anyway? I saw the pictures of you two on Instagram last week. Why are you trying to go after someone else?"

"I'm not going after Stone," Jillian declared so no one would go tell ER.

Vanessa contradicted, "But you just said—"

Jillian got louder and defended, "I said he's after me."

Vanessa said, "So I just need to text ER and tell him that you're entertaining his friend's advances."

Jillian glared at my sister like she wanted to choke her. I, on the other hand, was happy Vanessa was back to her old spunky self. She could handle Jillian so well. Jillian's red face showed her embarrassment, and because she was so cold to so many, none of us cared to take up for her.

Thankfully the guys came over and broke up all the tension. Skylar stayed stuck next to me even though Ford wanted to hang out with her. Finally he just turned around and walked toward the arcade.

"What is wrong with you? I really hope you are not letting a little inconspicuous pimple allow you to not have fun with a guy who wouldn't care if you had a face covered in them."

"You're being sweet, Victoria, but don't get it twisted. The first thing that attracted Ford and me to each other was our looks."

"Okay, and now it's something deeper," I told her.

"My girls are laughing at me, and I know his boys are laughing at him for being with a zit-faced girl."

I said, "Has he done or said anything to you to make you feel uncomfortable about your face?" She shook her head. "Then that's all the proof you need. But if breaking out makes you feel self-conscious, stay away from the sodas. You drink a ton of them, and during the teen years, the acid is not a friend to the face."

"I've been told that, but I'm so addicted to Coca-Cola."

She was right. We all knew that was her favorite drink. It was a wonder she hadn't turned into a Coke can.

"Thank you, though," she said, giving my hand an appreciative squeeze. "We got to get you somebody. Since your sister set Jillian straight about Stone, you should go for him. He is such a sweetheart and a hottie too."

But I doubted that Jillian was going to quit all the flirting just because she'd been called out on it. And sure enough, as soon as it was time to go, she was the first one grabbing Stone's hand. He didn't pull it away. If he was remotely interested in me, he wouldn't flaunt wanting to be with her all in my face when I was looking. For a white boy, with the firm butt he had, who wouldn't be looking? I just so happened to be right behind the two of them as we were all leaving. He opened the door and let her through it. It seemed like he was holding it for me, but as soon as I stepped toward the glass, he let go, and the heavy door quickly swung in my face.

"Ouch!" I hollered out.

"Oh, I'm sorry!" he said.

Irritated, I snapped, "Sure you are."

"I am. I didn't see you."

"Whatever, Stone. Fine."

Out in the parking lot, I was so angry. I wanted to be asleep, but my sister wanted to hang out more with her boyfriend. Steam was piping from my ears like I was a train engine. Finally, I went over and interrupted them.

"Why don't you just let Emerson take you home?" I asked her.

"You know I've got to ride home with you."

"Dad's back and your mom's in town. I'm ready to go."

Vanessa saw I was serious. She gave her boyfriend a kiss. She got in the car with me and slammed the door.

Quickly I said, "You can't be mad at me because I'm tired. It's almost twelve o'clock, and I've been up on my feet all night."

"I'm not mad at that. I just don't like people calling me dumb and being right about it. I don't want to get off focus. I want to get my life together and have some choices."

"Well, I don't mind helping you."

"You don't?"

"No, but you're in tutoring with Emerson, right?"

"Yeah, but it's hard to think about school books when I'm with the guy I like. You know what I'm saying? Nah, you don't know. You've never been in love."

"And you can't be in love either after two minutes."

"Ha-ha-ha. Not funny."

Still, she hugged me, and I could tell that she was extremely appreciative that I offered to help her. As soon as we walked in the house, Vanessa's phone rang. She went straight to her room. If love made you have to talk every five minutes, I wasn't interested. I went to tell my mom we were home.

"Wow, you just don't know how good you make me feel. Come on, baby, don't stop," I heard her seductively say.

What in the world was going on? Maybe that was my dad she was talking to inside the bedroom. But I hadn't seen my dad's car when we pulled in.

"All right, Dad. We'll be ready in the afternoon. Okay, see y'all at the competition," Vanessa said into her phone, walking past me.

"You're talking to Dad?" I asked when she hung up the phone.

"Yeah, and he wants you and me to go with him to take my mom and everybody back down to Twiggs County tomorrow evening. Cool?"

"Yeah, sure," I said, still not getting what was going on in my mom's room.

I guess my mom didn't hear us outside because she kept on with the extremely inappropriate conversation. I cracked the door to make sure no one else was in there with her. There wasn't, but she was on the phone talking real seductively to someone who obviously wasn't Dad. I wasn't crazy. I wasn't imagining this. Something was going on, and I made up my mind right then and there that I was going to figure it out. For the next few days my mission would be gathering evidence.

CHAPTER TWO

Shut Down

I was on the verge of a nervous breakdown, standing in the doorway of my mother's bedroom, hearing her talk in such a scandalous way to a man who wasn't my father. She was enjoying it, telling the man she wished he could do this, asking him to imagine her doing that. It was way too kinky, totally X-rated, and absolutely inappropriate for a mother and a wife to be saying, for goodness' sake.

What was up with her? What was her problem? Why did she think this was okay? And why did I have to be the one to find out about it? Was this my dad's fault? Had he put her on an emotional rollercoaster ride for so long that now she was ready to get off and ride with someone else? We had to talk about this thing, but as soon as I stepped in to say something, I was distracted by the conversation.

My mother was sitting on her bed like she was watching television. "I see you smiling through the phone. I know my touch feels good. We could have a good time, baby. Relax and enjoy it. Oh yeah, baby, talk to me."

She'd really lost her mind. My mom was totally relaxed. I was pulling my wavy hair out.

"Mom!" I finally shouted, unable to take any more. "What are you doing?"

"Uh ... I, I've gotta go," she said, tripping over her words as she slammed the phone down hard like it was a hammer driving a nail into wood.

The way that she was talking, the person on the other end probably thought she had on some type of negligee. She was still fully dressed in what she had on at the game. I was all confused, and she looked even more puzzled seeing me standing there.

"Victoria, honey, you startled me! I thought you and Vanessa went somewhere. You guys did so good tonight!" she said before I could get a word in.

She just kept talking about the game and about how excited she was for Vanessa that her mom and other siblings came.

"Where is Dad?" I asked with much attitude. "I thought you two had worked out everything; clearly not." I hoped she understood that I was alluding to the fact that I'd heard her on the phone and wanted her to know it. But if she got my drift, she didn't acknowledge it.

She just came over, hugged me real tight, and said, "Your dad and I are healthy, okay? We're taking our time. He's at the hotel with Junior tonight. He said he had a lot of things to talk about with Vanessa's mom."

"And you're okay with that, that he's not here?"

"Yeah, I had some work that I needed to do anyway."

I raised my eyebrows. What I'd heard her doing was all pleasure. Was she serious?

When she didn't seem to get the message, I said, "Mom, you've got to explain to me what you were just—"

Getting irritated, she huffed, "What do you mean? It's too late to talk about anything. Where'd you guys go anyway?" She was trying to take control of the conversation.

"We went to eat pizza."

"Well, honey, I hope you didn't eat too much of it," she said as she touched my stomach. "You don't want that gut to bulge."

There was no way my mom could have known how sensitive I was about my weight, but when she said that, I forgot all about why I stepped into her room to confront her. I didn't think she purposely meant to hurt my feelings, but the critical look on her face showed how concerned she was with my figure. My eyes started tearing up.

"How many pieces of pizza did you have, sweetie? You're really going to have to start working on your eating habits."

My mom was clueless to the fact that her words were demoralizing me. She just kept going on and on about how men didn't like fat women. Maybe she was an expert on what men liked, and I just didn't know it.

"Why are you crying?" she said when she finally noticed my tears.

"You're calling me fat."

"No, no, no, I said you need to watch it before you get fat. You're a cheerleader for goodness' sake. Sweetheart, you are not large. It's just that you have an image to uphold. Smaller portions of everything, that's what you need to be eating now. Some girls just gain more than others. You must have gotten this from your dad's side because I was thin all through high school and college."

Yeah, but she didn't graduate. She dropped out when she got pregnant with me. Her family joked that she had only gone to college to snag a baller, and it had worked. I couldn't be my mom. She was white with blonde hair. Though she'd never made me feel like I was ugly before, at that moment she was making me feel like I was disgusting to her. That was hard.

"I'm sorry I bothered you, Mom."

"It's okay, sweetie. You're never a bother. Just knock next time, okay?"

After the conversation that I'd just heard, she didn't have to tell me that. Once we said our goodnights, I ran straight to the bathroom. I had to get that food out of my system quickly.

I could feel the dough and cheese sticking to my ribs like glue does to paper. I needed to purge. I figured if Jillian could do it and still look so cute, I would be fine doing it too.

I got on my knees and lifted up the seat. I had to get this food out. I just didn't know how. Then I remembered Jillian's demonstration from earlier. I needed to stick my fingers down my throat. I tried with my index finger, but nothing happened. I stuck it down further. Still nothing. Then I stuck two fingers down as far as I could get them. I started gagging, and I knew that I was on the right track.

"Come on, come on, come on," I thought to myself.

I took my fingers out of my mouth to catch my breath, and then I stuck them back down my throat at full thrust. That did the trick. I leaned over as the food I recently ate came gushing out of my mouth. I sank down by the toilet. I was exhausted from the effort, but I knew that wasn't all of the food in my stomach. So I leaned back over the toilet, stuck my fingers in my mouth again, and made more of my dinner come out. I heard the door crack open, but I couldn't stop the vomit.

When I finally got things under control, I jerked back and saw Vanessa standing there looking at me.

"What did you just do?"

"Shut the door," I cried out.

"This isn't even your bathroom. I share this one with Junior. You have your own."

"Go, Vanessa, dang."

"Don't tell me to go away. What are you doing?"

"Please, just go away. I don't feel good."

"When you don't feel good, you don't need to have your hand in your mouth to throw up. Are you bulimic? Do we need to talk about this? Victoria, what's going on? You're tight. Don't let what those fools said tonight get to you. You are too sensitive."

Dropping my head, I profusely wiped my brow. "You don't understand. It's hard to be me. It's hard to fit in. It's hard to be perfect. Just mind your own business, okay?"

"No, it's not okay," she said, not letting me get around her to leave the bathroom.

"What do you want, Vanessa? What are you going to do?"

"I'm going to tell your mom, that's what."

Quickly, I leapt toward her. I caught hold of her arm and yanked it hard. She had to leave this be!

"Listen to me. My mom's got a lot going on right now. The last thing she needs to do is worry about me. Forget what you saw tonight. The food gave me an upset stomach. That's all. I just wanted to make sure I got it all out so I wouldn't be sick tomorrow. We have to get to the school early for the competition, remember? We're going out of town with Dad as well. I didn't want to have food poisoning or anything."

"Well, I'm fine from the pizza," she argued, letting me know she wasn't buying my story.

"You hardly ate any of it."

"Yeah, that's true," she said slowly, considering. "You sure that's all it is?"

I said yes, but my heart said no. Whatever was going on with me mentally, I could not explain it. Deep down, I wanted to contain it. But how?

Sensing that I was breaking, Vanessa hugged me. "I just care about you. You can talk to me about anything. We're sisters."

Her embrace felt great. It did not erase my issue, though. What I'd just done to myself felt horrible. However, I was thrilled the food couldn't settle and add to my weight. I was so off balance.

"Victoria! I thought you were up," Vanessa shouted as she pulled the covers back. "Your mom is ready to take us to the school. Coach Pat wants us there at eight o'clock. It's seven fifty-five. I don't want to run any bleachers. Get up, girl."

It was the annual Battle at the Grove, where Grovehill High School hosted a cheerleading competition. We had thirty-two teams set to compete, plus we were doing an exhibition. It was truly a battle because in each of the eight divisions—middle school, JV, co-ed, class-A, class 2A, class 3A, class 4A, and class 5A—there were four teams competing against each other for first, second, and third place.

The battle was serious because one team in each division would not get a trophy. It was brutal, but everyone loved coming to our competitions over the years because the best of the best around the state entered. And it gave teams a chance to see everyone's routines before state. We were going to do an exhibition so we could see where we were strong and weak.

"Okay, okay, just give me a few minutes," I said, feeling like a Mack truck had run me over.

"We don't have a few minutes. You need to grab your stuff and come on. I'll get you something to eat in the car."

"No!" I shrieked. "I don't want anything to eat."

"You got to eat something. You're going to be out there all day."

"I said no, okay? I'll be ready in a minute."

When I sat up to get out of the bed, I felt weak. There had never been a time when I hadn't kept my food down. I knew it was taking a toll on me. My stomach was growling. Yet I refused to eat breakfast. Somehow I was going to have to find a way to make it through the day without food. After I got out of bed, I went to the mirror and looked at myself.

I thought, "Victoria House, you can do this. You got a slamming GPA because you study. You made the competition team because you got the skills. You want to lose weight, girl? Nothing

to it but to do it. Don't even think about food."
When my stomach growled again, I said out
loud, "Don't even think about it."

Getting to the car last, I had no choice but
to get in the back. Vanessa was sitting up front
with my mom. Actually that was just fine with
me. The way they both looked at me, I hoped
they hadn't talked. My mom didn't need to tell
Vanessa that she thought I overheard her talking. With Vanessa's mom in town trying to get
her life together, the last thing my dad needed
was a reason to not want to be with my mom.
If my fast-tail mom was cheating, that was certainly a big reason.

I also didn't want Vanessa telling my mom
that she'd seen me throw up my food—not that
I'd be surprised if my mom didn't care. She'd
basically called me fat, after all. However, deep
down I truly felt my mom did care. If she knew I
was headed down the dangerous road I was on,
she would be trying to get me help or something.

My stomach growled loudly.

"Dang, girl, you better eat some of this."
Vanessa turned around and held out a chicken
biscuit.

"And you can have my orange juice," my mom chirped. It didn't seem like Vanessa had told her anything about me.

Vanessa knew chicken biscuits were my favorite breakfast food. I didn't know if she was really looking out for me or if she had fixed extras regardless of what I had brashly told her when she was in my room. Maybe she just made herself too many and was giving one to me out of pity to quiet my begging stomach. Either way, I realized I didn't need to stay away from food. I had a plan. When I got to the school, I wouldn't keep it down. So I took the biscuit from her and gobbled it up.

"I knew you were hungry," Vanessa said.

All the way to the school, I had to listen to my mom be all excited about Vanessa and her new boy. It's not like she was excited that Vanessa had gotten together with just any-body. My mom and dad loved the Prince family because Emerson's dad was the pastor of our church.

"I just can't believe this. You guys are officially together. I always thought that boy liked you."

"Really? You did?" Vanessa was so giddy.

"Yeah, when he was supposed to be reading the Bible, he was looking straight into your eyes. We'd be praying, and I'd see him checking you out."

"Lisa!" Vanessa said, embarrassed.

The two of them chuckled. That was nowhere near close to the kinky things my mom was saying lately. Vanessa thought that she was all great and stuff, but if she knew my mom was cheating on our dad, she wouldn't be as friendly. My sister would be livid.

I was past being jealous of the two of them getting close. I had my own issues, and I just really didn't feel like watching the two of them get along so great when I was so all over the map emotionally.

"Well, I'll be back later, and Dad's bringing your mom and everybody," my mom said to Vanessa.

Not feeling my best, I didn't want an audience. "You guys don't have to come. We're not even really competing today."

Vanessa wasn't having that. "No, come, Lisa. Ignore Victoria. I want everyone to come! I want my mom to see me. And try to get them here at the beginning. Tell Daddy not to be late. Not to brag, but our routine is definitely better than everyone else's."

When we got inside, we got chewed out because we were late.

"It's eight thirty and teams will be coming through the doors any minute. I need you guys to man your stations," our tough but cool cheer coach, Coach Pat, said.

His wife was our other cheer coach, and I wondered where she was. She was also one of our school counselors. As much as I didn't want to talk to anyone, deep down I knew I needed to.

"Is your wife around?" I asked him.

"She's around here somewhere, but I need you all to go find Jillian so you can help walk teams to their classrooms."

"I don't want to work with Jillian!" Vanessa protested.

I definitely didn't want to either. Jillian was so judgmental. But Coach wasn't giving us a choice.

He said, "You guys will be fine. All three of you were late, so the other assignments have already been taken. You have no other options."

As the team of the school hosting the cheer competition, our members had to help vendors set up, make sure the concession stand was running, get the mats ready, and greet the judges. We also had to have someone at the door. Usually booster moms did that. My mom got out of setting up because she signed up to help us break down instead. Also as hosts, we had to get each team into a classroom so that the members could put on their makeup, get dressed, and have team time.

Before we located Jillian, I was able to duck into the bathroom and purge without Vanessa finding out. Then about forty minutes later, most of the teams had arrived. Jillian had something negative to say about every single team that came to us. When a team from Columbus, Georgia, arrived, Jillian was the first one to laugh at the girls' outfits. They weren't wearing uniforms. They didn't look like the ideal cheer squad, but looks could be deceiving. I overheard a parent whisper to another parent that they were from a poor area. I saw Vanessa get a far-off look in her eyes, and I knew my sister was thinking about her hometown.

"Shorts and white T-shirts? That's the uniform? They obviously didn't get the memo that they need to have real cheerleading attire to be taken seriously," Jillian said, sounding arrogant. I glared at her, trying to mentally message her to be quiet, but she looked confused. "What? The economy hit them that bad in the projects?"

"Okay, wait a minute," Vanessa said to her. "You beg everybody in the world nowadays to buy you this and buy you that. Word is going around that the funds in your house aren't flowing as freely as they used to. The little rich girl might be poor herself."

I figured my sister was just taking a shot in the dark and didn't know what she was talking about. At least I thought that was the case, but when I saw Jillian's face, I realized maybe that was why the fake-blonde-headed chick had been so mean. She had her own struggles that no one knew about. She wasn't letting on that that was the case, but both my sister and I could see that Vanessa was on to something. From that point on, Jillian didn't say another negative word about anybody else. I learned from Vanessa that sometimes you've just got to tell people what's right so they stop being wrong.

"You're barely touching your Chick-fil-A sandwich," my sister said to me as the afternoon approached.

"Well, it's just that I ate in the car," I tried explaining.

"That was almost four hours ago, and you know we're about to go on in a little while."

Huffing, I said, "In another hour."

"You know if you don't have anything in your stomach, you'll be too weak to perform," my sister said, nagging me like she was my mom.

"I got it."

"Oh, here come the guys!" Jillian called out. Most of the cheerleaders had a guy, especially my friends and for sure my sister.

All their attention turned to the guys. It was actually perfect timing when they walked in. Other teams were competing, and Coach had given us a fifteen-minute break before we needed to start warming up for our exhibition performance. Nobody was paying me any attention, and the sandwich before me just seemed to be calling my name.

I imagined the sandwich saying, "Victoria, pick me up! Take a bite. You know you want to eat me. You know you want to gobble me up! Come on, I'm not going to put any pounds on you, and I really like to be eaten with fries and a Coke. We'll all get in your stomach and make you feel real good. Come on. Just take a bite!"

I shook my head. Was I going crazy? Obviously yes, to think a sandwich was talking to me. But when my stomach growled, I realized I had to do something. So I took a bite. Just one at first, but then another and another. Then before I knew it, I had devoured it all. Instantly, I regretted it and immediately felt like I was five pounds heavier. I found myself getting upset that the football players were there.

Skylar was being turned around by our running back, Ford. Though they were a cute couple, they didn't have to rub it in everybody else's face. It was like whatever they did, everybody else followed their lead. Ariel and Ryder weren't any better. They said they weren't dating, but every time you saw them, they were flirting.

Yaris and Hagen fussed more than any couple I knew. Something was going on with the two of them, and I made a mental note to ask Yaris about it. It wasn't like I could really give her any advice, though, because I was all alone.

Then I saw him. Stone, that tall, beautiful specimen of a man, was heading my way. I wiped my mouth. What was I going to say to him? What was he going to say to me? But Jillian popped in his face and smiled so wide that there was no way he could have noticed me. Embarrassed that I even wanted to talk to him, I dashed to the bathroom.

As soon as I got to the bathroom, I immediately went to the empty stall. I didn't get on my knees, but I leaned over, and without touching the toilet, put two fingers as far as they could stretch down my throat, and regurgitated. Just like I felt bad eating, I felt bad for doing that to my body because my stomach was going through all kinds of changes, as the food that just went down was now coming up. I was a big, fat pig. At least that's what my mind kept telling me. If doing this would help my waist look more like Jillian's, then I could deal with it. Then I heard giggling.

I had dashed into the bathroom so fast that I just now realized it was crowded with other girls. This was a private thing. I certainly didn't need anyone to know what I was doing. I already felt like the laughing stock because of my weight. I didn't need to be taunted because of my actions too.

I was getting a ton of stares when I came out of the stall, but thankfully they were from girls who went to other schools and didn't know me. Yeah, my red uniform identified me as a Grovehill cheerleader, but my mixed skin blended in with the skin tones of a bunch of girls from the other teams. They didn't know I actually caused myself to throw up. I could have really been sick. As I thought about it, I realized girls were so mean, cruel, and rude. Why were they laughing? But I couldn't be mad at anybody. I was making my own choices. I had an image in my mind that I was aspiring to. No pain, no gain, right?

When I went back over to where my team had been, everyone was gone. I tried to walk as fast as I could over toward the mats to warm up, but I felt queasy and weak, like I was about to keel over. I couldn't get to the water fountain fast enough. I splashed water on my face and drank some down.

Coach Joann came rushing up to me with a worried look. "You don't look so good. We've been looking for you. The girls are warming up. Are you okay?"

Now was my chance to talk to her. Now was my chance to tell her what was going on with me. Now was my chance to open up and get help. I mean, after all, she was a counselor. But I couldn't say a word. I clammed up and nodded meekly in response.

"You sure you're okay?"

I just nodded again and tried to pat the water from my face so I wouldn't mess up my makeup. As soon as we turned the corner, all of the guys were standing right there as we were working out. My half-wet face made me look like I was perspiring or something.

"I don't feel good," I finally said to her as I turned around and dashed away.

She quickly followed me. "Victoria, you're not pregnant or anything are you?"

"No, I just don't want them to see me looking like this."

"You look beautiful. What are you talking about?"

"I do not. Don't lie."

"Victoria! I wouldn't ever tell you something I didn't truly believe."

She reached in her pocket and pulled out some tissue. "Can I just dab your face?" she said as I jerked back.

When she tried again, I finally stood still and let her help clean me up. She was such a beautiful woman. I admired that. I wanted to be like her one day and have a man who loved me as much as her husband clearly loved her. Not that I needed a man to be there, but if I had to have one, I certainly wanted him to treat me how Coach Pat treated her.

"I'll be fine."

"All right," she said, giving me a hug.

When we went back over to the mats, our team had already gone into the gym. We were on deck to go in for our performance. Coach caught me up with them.

Jillian was part of my stunt group. I had to help lift her into the air. I was one of her bases. The problem was that of all the four stunt groups, ours was the most unreliable. Jillian loved to blame me, but she didn't know how to hold her weight.

"Don't drop me," Jillian turned and said to me in a threatening way.

"Just go out there," Vanessa said, once again having my back.

My sister smiled at me, but I couldn't smile back. Not because I didn't want to or because I wasn't grateful that she was there, but because once again, I felt so tired. A full-on cheer routine was the last thing I needed to be doing, but I couldn't let anyone down. When we went out there, both sides of the bleachers were full of spectators there to support their teams. But the pressure was on because everyone knew we were supposed to be really good. Nervousness set in as if I was about to take the SAT or some big test my college acceptance depended on.

When the music started, I could barely keep up with the fast pace. Thankfully my instincts kicked in. We'd done the number so many times that it was second nature, even though I was a little out of it.

However, when we had to lift Jillian up on the first stunt, I was wobbly. We cradled her down, and because we had such difficulty pulling it off, people in the stands were getting to their feet and clapping. All of the noise and stomping didn't help to settle me. I really wanted them to shut up, but I kept going. It was time to lift Jillian up again, but I couldn't hold her weight, and she came tumbling down on top of me.

"What the heck, Victoria?" Jillian screamed. "You could have killed me! You—"

"Don't you yell at her, you crazy—" Vanessa butted in.

"Don't you dare call me any names, sista!" Jillian screeched.

Just then, the whole team was fussing with each other instead of showing off, which was what we set out to do. Our routine had become a joke of a performance. My team shut down.

CHAPTER THREE

Hang On

Girls! What in the world was that all about?"
Coach Pat said to me and Vanessa as soon as we
got off the floor.

We were supposed to be the hostesses on our
best behavior. We were supposed to be the model
cheerleaders for the day. We had completely
embarrassed ourselves on both accounts.

"Don't look at us," Vanessa boldly defended.
"It's all Jillian's fault. She can't handle her
weight, but she gets mad at my sister about it."

"Your sister? Are you kidding? You guys are
half sisters. You don't even have the same mom,
and you were born the same year. It's pathetic.
I'm just saying," Jillian said as many of the girls

started huffing and puffing, looking over at her like she had lost her mind. "What? I'm just saying what everybody else is thinking around here. Everyone's been talking about the fact that it just came out there is a brother their same age."

"You know what?" Vanessa said as she stepped into Jillian's face. "Whole sister, half sister, adopted sister, play sister, you're just jealous that you don't have any sisters. No one cares enough about you to have your back."

Vanessa's advance sent Jillian running behind the coach. "Do you see the barracudas I have to deal with on this team?" she whined to him.

He just looked at her like she was crazy. I heard all this around me and was aware of the drama, but I felt so weak. I just needed to sit down before I collapsed.

"What do we do now, Coach?" Skylar said to him.

Coach said, "We've got to hand out awards to people. We've got to go back out there. This isn't about a few girls tussling; this is about all of us. Vanessa, Jillian, can you guys please keep it together for the sake of the team?"

"She's bad-mouthing my family, and you think I'm just supposed to let it go? I'm sick of her scrawny behind," my sister vented.

"All right, Vanessa. I'm tired of hearing all of you girls! I'm going to leave y'all in here for three minutes, and you better work it out, or regional and state are off," Coach told us in a serious tone.

Coach Pat stepped out of the room, but his wife didn't go anywhere. "Listen, girls, I know it's been a long season. We're around each other all the time, and y'all have so much going on. But we don't need to fall apart now."

"We just did fall apart," Yaris cried.

"That's okay, Yaris," Coach Joann said. "If we go back out there as one, we can overcome the embarrassment. We'll get to work preparing for the next competition, and we'll blow every-one away. We'll get ready for regional, and we'll work this out so we can win state. Adversity can make you stronger, and that's what we need to do right now. You girls have to rise up and hang in there. Victoria," she said, calling my name. I guess I was looking somewhere else. "You look like you're about to pass out, sweetie."

"Well, that's what happened when we were competing. She didn't even lift me up," Jillian added. "You didn't do your part."

"I'm sorry. I'm just tired," I managed to say.

"You don't have to apologize to her behind. I'm going to go find our folks," Vanessa said, clearly worried about me as well.

When Vanessa went to find our parents in the stands, I was actually surprised that a lot of the cheerleaders came around me and tried to make sure I was okay. Skylar handed me water, Ariel got me Gatorade, and Yaris rubbed my back. I didn't want them making a big fuss over me, but I was too drained to tell them to stop.

"Oh my goodness, Victoria, let's get you home," my mom said when Vanessa brought our parents over.

"No, you've got to help clean up, and I gotta stay with the team cause we're gonna ..." I couldn't even finish my sentence.

"No arguments. It's time for you to go and relax, girl," my dad said, helping me up.

When I looked up, Emerson was asking me if I was okay. I remember my mom standing there. Was I going crazy? I had to be because I didn't even realize I wasn't in the gym anymore. I was walking out toward the front door.

When I wobbled, Emerson caught me. I saw Vanessa staring, so I quickly tried to pull myself away from him. "I'm fine. You can let go of me," I said to Emerson, even though I was pretty frail.

I was out of it, but I wasn't an idiot. I did not need any issues with Vanessa. Emerson let go of me and went and took Vanessa's hand.

"Oh, he's cute, honey," Vanessa's mom said to her, coming up behind us with her other children and my brother.

As I stumbled again, a different pair of strong arms caught me. "I got you."

Like a superhero saving the day, Stone was there. I was so embarrassed. I really didn't want him touching me at all, pretending to be sweet on me when he was really into Jillian. But I needed the assistance.

"Mom, can you just hurry up and take me home please?" I asked.

"If you want to stay for the end of this thing, I can bring you home," Emerson said to Vanessa.

"Could you do that?" my mom said, not wanting Vanessa to have to leave because of me. "I really want to go home with Victoria and make sure she's all right."

I didn't know if that was the truth or if my mom wanted to hurry up and get home to get back on the phone with her guy friend. Vanessa seemed unsure. Knowing the girls on our team as I did, I knew they wouldn't appreciate both of us leaving.

I turned to my sister and said, "You stay."

"But, Dad, when are you taking them home?" Vanessa asked.

"We're going to check out of the hotel and get their things. We'll come by the house, swoop you guys up, and keep it moving. I want you girls to meet your brother on this trip. And I want to meet him too."

"Victoria needs to rest," my mom said.

I wanted to say, "Victoria can speak for herself." If all I'd be doing was driving a couple of hours, that was resting. I did want to meet my brother, and, honestly, I wanted to get away.

Vanessa conceded. "Dad, we'll be done with everything in a couple of hours, and I'll be at the house."

Stone helped me to the car. I was too tired to even tell him thanks. I didn't know what needing an IV felt like, but I could not imagine it being much different from the way I felt.

My mom drove me and Junior back to our house. I wanted to relax and take it easy, but my mom was asking a million questions. Yet, she was the one who needed to be interrogated.

She said, "I just don't think you need to be going on any long trips right now. You'd be so faint and dizzy. Do we need to go to the emergency room? To the urgent care center?"

"No, Mom, I'm fine. You can come along to make sure I'm okay," I said, knowing I was forcing her hand.

"There's not enough room in your dad's car. Vanessa's mom, her three other children, you and Vanessa, plus your dad ... that's okay. Besides, your brother's got some stuff going on tomorrow that I have to be there for. He's trying out for his school basketball team."

Junior excitedly said, "That's right!"

My mom helped me lie down in my room to get a couple hours of rest. I really could tell she loved me, but if she cared so, why was she breaking up our family? Maybe if I got my dad alone when we were away, I'd be able to get him to understand that my mom needed some affection. But just like my mom didn't really understand what was going on with me, I didn't know what was going on with her either. Maybe she had a real reason for doing what she was doing.

When she came back with some hot tea for me to sip on, I said, "I love you."

"I love you too, baby," she said. "Everything is gonna be okay."

I hugged her tight, believing it. We were the strong House family. Now I just needed us to be a loving home.

He wrapped his strong arms around me and pulled me close. His breath felt warm and wonderful on my neck, and I let my hair flow in the breeze. I leaned back, enjoying every minute of his touch. As the breeze blew stronger around us and I started to shiver from the storm, he pulled me real close and held me tight. His heart was pounding through his chest, and it spoke to me, saying, "You are safe." He was so much taller than me. He rested his chin on my head, and then he touched my chin and lifted it up toward his face. Our eyes were connected. Our hearts were in sync. But just as our lips touched, I awoke.

There sat Vanessa by my bed. I was dreaming the whole time. Startled by her presence but scared that I was thinking of Stone, I tried to keep it together. To straighten myself out, I wiped my brow.

I asked, "What are you doing here? Why did you scare me like that? Did I miss Dad? Is he ready to go?"

"I was watching over you, and I think I figured this out."

"What are you talking about?"

"I know what's wrong with you. We were at the cheerleading meet eating, folks were talking about you eating, and someone said you dashed off to the bathroom. Next thing you know, you're weak, sick, and tired. You threw up again, didn't you?"

"What are you talking about?" I asked, feigning indignation so she wouldn't know she had it right.

"You can't do that."

"I'm okay. I'm fine. I don't know what you're thinking—"

"I just told you what I'm thinking," Vanessa said, cutting me off. "And don't deny it. I saw you last night, and you did the same thing today. You told me you ate something bad; I knew that wasn't the case. You're bulimic. Or you're new at it, and you're trying to be. Sis, you're not doing a good job. You're gonna end up in the hospital or something—girl, are you crazy? Does your mom know?"

Vanessa turned around to head out of the room and tell her. I jumped out of my bed and grabbed her arm. "Please, I'm dealing with some stuff, okay?"

"So you're admitting it? You purposely threw up last night, and you did the same thing today."

"I'm not admitting anything. I'm just saying, just … chill. Leave me alone, please."

"Girls, are y'all ready to go?" I heard our dad call out.

"Please don't say anything. You're going to be with me tonight and tomorrow. You'll see I'm not harming myself in any way."

"When was the last time you ate anything, Victoria?"

"My mom fixed me some tea."

"The only way I'm not saying anything is if you let me fix you a peanut butter and jelly sandwich, and I see you keep it down."

I threw my hands up in the air. I knew my sister loved me. It was hard to put anything past her, so I just agreed. Changing my shirt, I looked in the mirror and was again disgusted by the fat and flab in my stomach area. I'd told Vanessa I was going to eat her little sandwich, but I was going to have to find a way around that. If I didn't figure out a way to reverse the direction my body was going, I wouldn't be able to fit into any cheerleading uniform next year because they wouldn't have one big enough. The last thing I wanted was cheerleading taken away because I did love it. I loved that it symbolized beauty, spunk, sass, and class. Currently, I felt none of those things. I needed help.

My mom peeked in the room and said, "Are you feeling okay to go?"

"I can stay," I said, wondering what she'd think of that.

"Well, your dad really wants you to go and see your grandma and meet your brother and all."

I figured she didn't want me around, even though she and I still had not directly addressed the fact that I caught her on the phone talking all sexy to some man who wasn't her husband. While she might not be sure I heard, she had a pretty good idea I probably did. That was the elephant in the room that neither of us wanted to deal with.

"All right, Mom, I'll give them some time. Thanks," I said as I hugged her real tight. "Thank you for tucking me in and caring and stuff. It was really nice."

"Sure, baby," she said as she kissed my cheek.

"I hope you and Dad are really trying to work things out."

"Of course we are."

"It takes two, ya know, Mom."

"I know that, baby. Now go, don't worry about me. Everything's okay, really."

As soon as we got in the car, Vanessa was in her element. I actually enjoyed sitting and talking to her sisters and brother. We were packed tight in my dad's Infiniti. I drifted off to sleep. I was awakened by a bunch of giggles, and it wasn't coming from the kids in the car. It was my dad and Vanessa's mom. He was attracted to her once before, enough to have a kid. Were they rekindling the fire? I started coughing.

"You okay?" Vanessa's mom asked me.

In my mind I said, "Heck no! You need to quit flirting with my father. He is married." But then my phone vibrated. It was a text from Vanessa, who was sitting beside me.

Her text read, "Chill out. Nothing's going on between our dad and my mom. I see you looking at them all suspicious and stuff. My mom's been depressed for a long time, and this is the first time she's been happy in a while. They're just friends, so no worries."

I texted back, "K."

I couldn't even look at my sister, and I didn't know how I felt about her being so in my head. It was like we were twins or something. But I did appreciate her putting me at ease. Finally, we got to her mom's house. The house looked like it was very old and on its last leg. The sight of it got to me. It looked bad *and* it was night. I couldn't imagine what it looked like during the day. I squeezed my sister's hand. I could tell she was embarrassed for me to view it. I was happy that she now lived in better conditions than the wretched little home before us.

"You're not going to stay with us?" her youngest sister asked in the most precious voice.

"No, we're going to go visit some people. I got to see my grandma and stuff, but hopefully I'll see you soon, okay?" Vanessa said, visibly trying to hold in her sadness.

Vanessa walked everyone to the door. It was just me and my dad for a moment. We both stared at the surroundings. There were grown men out with brown bags in their hands and held up to their mouths. Trash was all along the street.

"Rough life down here, huh?" my dad commented, reading my mind.

"Yes, sir," I said, really hating that anyone had to live in such a desolate place.

"I know it's been tough for you having Vanessa at home with us, but—"

"No, no, I'm glad she lives with us."

"I know you are, sweetie. Her mom's going to get it together."

"But if she does, Vanessa's not going to have to move back here, will she?"

"Your sister is getting older now. I don't want her to move back here, but I don't want to keep her from her mom either, ya know? We just have to hold on and see."

Watching Vanessa's sisters, brother, and mom tear up as she was about to leave them made me real sad. Was being in a bigger house better than being in a home full of love? Would I lose my sister just when we were starting to connect?

For the first time ever, I realized what Vanessa was giving up to live with us. I wasn't the only one who needed her. They needed her too. Clearly she was torn, and it was hard for me to see her breaking. When my dad got out to say bye to her mom, I opened up the car door, and Vanessa rushed inside the car to get away from her sadness. I held her tight.

"This is so hard, Victoria," she said, her voice somber.

"I know, I know. But it's going to be okay."

"How? How is it going to be okay when I live so good and I know they live like this ..."

"Come on, girls, let's get going," our dad said in a chipper voice as he got back in the car, trying to break up the melancholy. "They'll be fine."

Vanessa and I released our embrace. Neither of us was sure his statement would prove true. However, at that moment, all we could do was believe he was right and that life would get better.

We drove about ten minutes to a slightly better part of town. My grandmother had land. When we got to her house, she was so ecstatic to see my dad and Vanessa. Seeing me, on the other hand, was a different story.

Squinting her face, she said, "Well, who's this?"

It wasn't like she didn't know me. It had been a couple years since she'd seen me. I felt she was a little over-the-top in letting me know I felt like a stranger.

"It's me, Grandma," I said.

"And who is that?" she responded.

"Mom, this is Victoria," my dad said in a displeased voice.

"Oh yeah, the one who doesn't get down here much to see her grandma, huh? How you doing? Come on in! You sure have grown. But you're a skinny thing," she said, twirling me around.

Had I done something to this lady? Sure, I had my license, but I did not own a car. It wasn't as though I could come down to see her whenever. What did she expect?

As if reading my mind, she said, "You know you could pick up the phone to call your grandma once in awhile."

I wanted to say, "The telephone works on your end too."

After all, she was my grandma. How many birthday presents had I ever gotten from her? How many Christmas cards or gifts had she sent to me? If we felt like strangers, she needed to own up to her part of that. She was the adult, but I knew what the problem was. My mom felt uncomfortable around her because my grandmother and her sisters called my mom the devil. She was the one who took my father away from this seemingly godforsaken town. My grandma's house was one of the best ones I'd seen as we were driving around the area.

It was awkward. I could tell Grandma wanted to catch up with Vanessa and Dad, so I said, "Where can I put my things?"

Scornfully, my grandma said, "My own grandchild don't even know her way around my house. I tell you what, Vanessa, show the girl where to go."

Vanessa nodded respectfully. My sister put her arm in mine, trying to help me hold it together. We walked down the hall.

"She sure hates me," I said once we were out of earshot.

"Granny's tough."

I said, "Yeah, and rough and gruff, like the big bad wolf or something. I'm scared to go to sleep in here. I'm one of her grandchildren, and she's making me feel like I don't belong here."

"Well, just don't act uncomfortable around her. That will make it worse."

"I can't act all fake like we're best buddies. She's made it clear that's not the case. She gives you and Dad this big hug, and then she sees me, and the only thing she can talk about is my size."

"She didn't, though."

"Oh, come on, Vanessa," I sighed.

"Victoria, don't be so sensitive about this. You are just right."

"No, I'm being dead-on accurate about it. You know it, and that's why you came to my defense, which I appreciate. But it's just hard. I used to hate that my mom didn't want to bring us down here to see her, and now I don't want to be here," I said, plopping down on the bed. I felt like I weighed four hundred pounds or something.

"Well, come on, let's just get in our pj's, and we can talk to her some. She's really funny."

"I'll pass," I said as Vanessa went back out of the room we were sharing.

It was a guest bedroom, but there were pictures on the walls of my dad when he was younger. It took me a moment to realize it must have been his old room. I changed my clothes, got on my knees, and said a prayer. I had much to be thankful for. Life wasn't perfect, but it could have been worse. I was about to get in the bed when I realized I'd forgotten to brush my teeth. When I cracked the door to go out to the hall bathroom, I was stunned to hear my grandmother talking about me to my sister.

"It just seems weird. I don't have any connection to my other granddaughter."

"Grandma, give her a chance. Really, she's awesome."

"I just wish her mother hadn't kept me away

from her. Now she's all grown up, and I'm just supposed to ..."

She didn't even finish her sentence. She walked away. My sister leaned up against the hallway wall, hurting for what she'd just heard, but it was even worse for her when I walked out with wet eyes. My sister tried to comfort me, but I didn't want her compassion.

"She'll come around, Victoria."

"Tomorrow can't come soon enough, Vanessa, so I can leave. How 'bout that?"

I went to the bathroom and closed the door tight. When I came out of the bathroom, my dad had some other bags in his hands. Apparently he'd been outside when his mother was ragging on me. He could tell something was wrong with me, but I didn't want to talk about it.

"What's going on, babe? I'm so glad you're down here, and I know my mom is too."

"I doubt that," I said, being real.

"Did my mom say something to you?"

"Dad, just ... just let me go to sleep."

"And she wonders why I don't bring you guys down here more. I'll say something to her."

"Dad, please. You'll make it worse. She's my grandma. If she's supposed to love me, she will."

"I know she loves you."

"I'm glad you know that, but it doesn't matter," I informed him, before hurrying to change the subject. "I saw your baby pictures. You were so cute. I'll be okay. Goodnight, Dad."

"Goodnight, baby," he said as he kissed my forehead.

The next morning, I awoke to the best-smelling breakfast my nose had ever been around. I might have had an issue with the way my grandmother treated me, but I certainly did not have any problem with the way she cooked. Thick and buttery hot cakes; long, crispy bacon; fluffy, light eggs; and a few other goodies were on the table, all looking delicious. How in the world was I going to eat in moderation?

"Oh my gosh, Grandma. This looks yummy!" my sister exclaimed, coming in behind me. I had taken too long to give my grandma a compliment.

"You think so?" she said, melting when Vanessa said what I was thinking. "Go on, Victoria child, quit staring at it. Sit down, and let's eat."

As bad as I wanted to tear into it, I used will power. The problem was that my restraint made my grandma think I did not like her cooking, which was absolutely not the case. Inside I was dying to devour it. I wanted to take my time so I wouldn't eat too much, but she was insulted.

My dad leaned in and said, "Victoria, honey, you need to eat a little something."

"I'm watching my weight, Dad, okay?" I said.

He lifted his hands in the air as if in surrender, and I could see he wasn't going to argue with me. But when I saw my grandmother pouting, I allowed myself to finish the plate. I just didn't get up for seconds and thirds, as much as my stomach desired it. If I had to keep this meal down, I wasn't going to eat too much. But it was hard not to want more.

An hour later, I was thankful I'd escaped the table without consuming too much. My dad, Vanessa, and I were on the way to meet my brother. Though I didn't know how that would go, I was happy to get away from our grandmother's place. Maybe I'd write her a letter and tell her all about me. Maybe I'd ask her why she was so mean.

Maybe I'd apologize for the disconnect between us. I didn't know how I'd fix this or even if it could be fixed, but I did know deep down inside that there was no use avoiding the problem if I wanted things to be better between us.

"Does he know that we're coming?" Vanessa asked.

I would have never thought to ask that question, because certainly our brother had to know we were coming. However, my dad didn't say anything. He started adjusting his collar. We could see he hadn't told the boy. Vanessa and I gave each other a look. We knew to hold on.

"Okay, I think the house is right here."

It was the weirdest thing. There was a young man outside dribbling a basketball. Judging from his young, handsome dark face, he was about sixteen. He looked so much like a younger version of our father it was scary.

"That's him, Dad, right there," Vanessa said, again reading my mind.

"Yeah, I know. I see him," our dad said in a somber tone.

"Well, he's looking over here at the car wondering what we're doing in front of his house. We got to get out. We got to say something," Vanessa told our dad.

"Maybe I should come back alone," he said, second-guessing himself. "I'm taking you guys back to my mom's house, and I'll come pick you up later."

Not wanting to endure my grandmother again so soon, I opened the door. "Come on, Dad, we're already here."

"I don't even know the boy's name," my dad said in a melancholy voice as he opened his door.

"Can I help you guys?" The boy on the driveway said as he stood tall just like my father.

"You girls stay here," my dad told us.

My dad walked over to the young man. From what we could overhear, our brother was not happy to see our father.

"Like I want you to be a part of my life. Are you serious? I don't need no dad. I heard about you, Big Baller, Shot Caller. You can't even take care of your responsibilities. My grandma had to raise me after my mom died of a broken heart. Get off our property. Go!" the angry teen yelled out.

My dad dropped his head. I understood how the guy could be angry. I also knew that as much as none of us wanted this to be our life, we did have a dad who cared. He'd just found out about this boy, and he deserved a chance to be a father to him. My sad dad came back toward the car.

"I'm about to go give him a piece of my mind," Vanessa said, but my dad held her back.

He hugged us both in his arms as he looked back at the boy. "No, no, just leave him alone. I told him I loved him. I'll just leave him with that. I hope that he'll come around. Until then, I'll just hang on."

CHAPTER FOUR
Deeply Hurt

My house was so dismal that I was actually excited to go to school Monday morning. It wasn't just getting colder outside, it was getting real cold in our home. I think everyone but Junior had issues. My dad was hurt that his newfound son didn't accept him. Vanessa was broken-hearted that she was living better than the rest of her family. I still hated my body, and I was obsessed about how I could make myself throw up as quickly as possible after eating. And my mom … who knew what was going on with her? Yep, school was the only place where I thrived. It was my sanctuary.

Ms. Upshaw was my literature teacher. I had a ninety-eight in her class, and I generally enjoyed the work. But that day we had to write the first draft of the group papers we'd been assigned the week before. I was in a group with Emerson and Stone. I volunteered to write up the first draft using the research they'd sent me, if they handled the cover page. The two of them began to talk while they worked. I listened to some of their conversation.

"If your dad wants you to go on the tour, go to one concert. It's a teachers' workday tomorrow, so we don't have school. Go, man," Emerson encouraged him.

"Whatever, man. It's not like he makes it to any football games."

Emerson cut Stone a harsh glare, like he was crazy. "Uhh, because he's been working. Quit tripping, and just go and support your pops."

"I just don't like that he always wants things to be his way."

"Oh, and you don't?" Emerson said, calling Stone out.

Stone shook his head, and obviously there was more that he wasn't saying. "Whatever, man. You don't understand."

"I do understand. Parents are crazy; I get

that. When I dug deep with my dad, I realized I'd actually misunderstood him. His sense of reality was so distorted that he didn't even understand his own circumstances. Thankfully it wasn't what I thought either. If your dad doesn't know he's missing the mark with you, you have to show him."

"I don't know what you're talking about," Stone said.

I actually didn't know what Emerson meant either. Pastor Prince was the best man in our town. What could he have done to upset his son? Emerson looked up at me to see if I was listening, and I quickly put my eyes down.

He leaned in a little closer to Stone and said, "I thought my dad was cheating."

Stone almost laughed. "The reverend? Nah, man. That's my pops, in a hotel room with a different woman every other night, I'm sure."

Emerson reiterated, "I said I *thought* my dad was. The point is I was angry and upset with him, and I didn't give him the full benefit of the doubt. You may think you know how your dad rolls, but until you're in his world and can clearly see it, you can't be sure. At least let him know how much you need him, or he might not get it."

"You guys are doing an awful lot of talking over there," Ms. Upshaw said, her eyes on the three of us in the corner.

"Sorry, Ms. Upshaw," Stone said in his charming manner that seemed to come so naturally. He was such a ladies' man. But she pointed to the work and stayed on him.

"Don't give me any excuses. Just get the work done. This isn't something you can finish up for homework. I need the first draft of your papers by the end of class today. Get to writing."

While they were talking, I'd written most of it. I showed it to the two of them. Emerson nodded and grinned. Stone tried to bat his eyelashes my way, but I was done with all of that. I wasn't falling for him.

Truthfully, I wanted to connect with Emerson. I knew I wanted to talk with him about my situation and maybe see how everything in his world worked out, but I didn't want to bring that up in front of Stone. Plus Ms. Upshaw was watching us closely. So, shielding my phone from her view, I looked through it, found Emerson's number, and texted him.

"Hey, I need to talk to you after class. It's really important. I got some stuff on my heart that I need to share. It seems like only you can help me. I need you. Please."

I wondered why Emerson wasn't looking at his phone. Yes, I got that he had to put the final touches on the paper with Stone, but it would only take a second. I needed to make sure he understood how important it was that I talked to him right after class, so I sent him another text.

"Is it okay for us to talk after class? It's real important, and I do need you."

As soon as we turned in the paper, the bell began ringing. I tried to wait around for Emerson outside the door, but he just kept on talking to Stone and was slow to leave. They were like two cackling hens. Goodness, what was there left to say? I figured they wouldn't take that much longer. Both of them needed to get to class, but I needed to talk to Emerson ASAP. He had to help me figure out this thing with my mom.

Without realizing it, I was actually smiling

as I stood there in the hall waiting for Emerson to come out. I so needed to talk to him. Hearing that he'd thought his dad was having an affair, only to find out that that wasn't the case, gave me hope. I needed to see if maybe I'd somehow read my mom wrong too.

Then I got a text from him. It read: "You said you need me?"

I texted back: "Yes. I really need you."

All of a sudden, my sister startled me as she touched me on my back and said, "Who are you waiting on?"

"Oh, nobody."

"What do you mean nobody? You have this class with Emerson. Did he come out?"

"Umm ..."

"Has he come out? Yes or no? You're holding something back."

"Well, I was just ..."

"You were waiting on him," Vanessa said, calling me out.

"Well, yeah, but I need to ..."

This was so confusing. I didn't know how I was going to explain to her what I needed to ask Emerson. I just felt it was better that she didn't know, but she somehow figured it out and seemed angry about it.

Emerson came out of the door.

"Hey, lady," he said to her. "You ready?"

"No, I'm going to talk to my sister. You keep going."

And then he was gone.

"You seem disappointed," she said to me.

"I am disappointed," I told her truthfully. "I texted him during class about needing to talk to him, and he responded back. But just now he acted like he didn't have any intention of talking to me at all."

I started to follow him so I could ask what the deal was, but she stood in my way. This was important. She needed to move.

"Why are you looking at me like that?" I said to my sister when I could tell she was really getting upset.

"Why are you looking like you want to follow my man?"

"I just … um …" No way could I tell her.

"Quit trying to act like you don't even know what I'm talking about," she said. Then she whipped out his phone from her pocket and showed me my texts. "What kind of crap is this, Victoria? Of all people, I never thought my sister would be trying to take my guy. It really, really hurts me that you would go after him when you know we're together."

"No, you got it all wrong."

"Please! Don't even stand here and deny it. You're texting him in the middle of class—a class that you two are in together. I guess you were sitting there making goo-goo eyes at him or something?"

"No, and why are you getting loud, Vanessa? There's a logical explanation."

"Okay, great. Tell me what it is. Why would you be texting my man that you need him? I saw your text messages 'cause he left his phone with me, and I asked if I could leave my class early so I could be right here when y'all got out. And sure enough, I catch my sister standing here smiling like she's got some big plan waiting to talk to him."

"No, no, no, really, you got it all wrong."

"Yeah, I got it wrong, thinking you and I could be close. Thinking we could be tight. As soon as I'm not looking, you're going after the one thing that's been making me happy."

I tried to touch her arm, but she jerked it away. I needed her to calm down, but she kept getting louder. I needed her to listen to me, but she just kept talking.

Finally I said, "All right! Believe whatever you want to believe, dang it!" I dashed to the bathroom, completely broken.

I was so glad when the school day was over because it had been a rough one. Not because of the work, but because of the island it felt like I was on. Vanessa was pretty popular. She didn't think people marched to the beat she set. She was wrong. She was a leader. Heck, I even liked following her. I tried to meet her after each of her classes to explain she had things all wrong, but she wasn't giving me the time of day.

A part of me wanted to go find Emerson so I could explain all this nonsense, and he could help me clear it up. Surely he knew that I didn't have the hots for him, and if in confidence I told him what was going on, which is what I planned to do anyway because I needed his advice, he'd probably be able to talk some sense into her. Finally, at the end of the school day I bumped into him right before he went into the boys' locker room to change for football practice.

"Hey, can I talk to you for a sec?" I said.

"Yeah, sure, what's up?"

I motioned for him to come closer to me. What I had to tell him was extremely personal. I mean, I couldn't just blurt out that I thought my mom was having an affair to the whole school without having my business posted all over some Internet site the next second. I just couldn't take that chance, but his version of coming close was not the same as mine. He didn't budge. Had my sister talked to him during the day and made him think I liked him or something? Did I have bad breath? Just as I was about to tell him I wasn't going to bite him, Yaris and Ariel walked by.

Ariel said loudly, "Darn! I guess Vanessa was telling the truth."

"I know, right? She's all close to him," Yaris mock-whispered.

They rolled their eyes my way. Then they walked into the girls' locker room. Emerson heard it too, and he seemed to be real uncomfortable.

"Never mind. Forget it," I said to him.

"Okay, see you," he said, looking happy to be off the hook.

Why didn't he just say "I have a girlfriend already" so I could say "Don't flatter yourself"? I was so bummed. I needed his advice, but he'd really ticked me off.

I went in the locker room and marched up to Yaris. "Yaris, what is going on? Why all the whispering about me under your breath?"

"What are you talking about?" she said, trying to blow me off.

"Ariel?" I said, turning to my other so-called friend. But Ariel didn't even respond. She just flipped her blonde hair, turned back to the locker, and started dressing for practice.

"Oh, so you're gonna act like I'm not standing here? You two make a big scene and everything, but nobody can talk to me? It's like that?"

Skylar came hustling into the locker room and said, "Did you guys hear about—"

Then she saw me and stopped talking.

Broken-hearted, I said, "Why don't you finish what you were about to say?"

"Why don't you stop bothering everybody?" my sister interjected, coming around the corner.

I don't know what hurt me worse: that they instantly believed whatever my sister told them about me when we were all supposed to be tight, or that they wouldn't give me a chance to explain. Having them believe the worst without even hearing my side of the story was hard. If it had to be like that, though, screw them.

I got dressed so fast you'd have thought they were handing out a prize for the first cheerleader to the mat or something. In reality, I didn't want to be around the girls. If Vanessa had them believing her lies, I certainly wasn't going to sit there and beg for them to hear me out.

I just hated that while I was trying to hold my family together, my secrecy ended up adding to my personal downward spiral. Coach Joann was already out in the gym, sitting alone on the bleachers looking at her clipboard. She smiled my way and asked if I was okay. Once again I said yes.

I didn't mean to. I didn't want to. I didn't try to. She was a counselor. Couldn't she tell I was down, desolate, and depressed? She knew the routine. Normally at practice I was always with my girls. Now I felt like a skunk, a stinky girl who was trying to steal her sister's man.

At least I was feeling better physically, because mentally, I was exhausted. I wasn't used to staying in my own little world during cheerleading practice. We were one big, happy family, but Vanessa let her suspicions leak about me, and everyone stayed her distance. Even the two freshmen on the squad gave me the cold shoulder, and those girls normally followed me around like puppy dogs. I guess that was when they thought I was part of the in-crew, and now that I wasn't a savvy girl, one who they deemed knew it all, was liked by all, and had it all going on, they were staying away from me.

Coach had broken the routine up into parts. We'd practiced the cheer, we'd practiced the dance part, and now we had to practice the stunts and tumbling.

He said, "You know what, bring it in, girls, because before you guys practice stunting, we need to talk. I was going to let it go. My wife told me sometimes you girls have your squabbles, but I'm your coach, and we have a state competition on the line. Just because we won last year doesn't mean we have it on lock. You guys having attitudes, issues, and problems with each other, that comes across to the judges. You might not think people pick up on your eyes rolling, your necks going, and your hips swaying like you're ready to knock somebody out, but it's noticeable. When we started the season, we talked about one season, one team, and one goal. We were all in. Put the drama aside. Talk to my wife if you need to, but leave that stuff somewhere else because when it comes time for us to lift each other up, have each other's backs, and take care of business, you guys got to be focused. You guys have to act like a team."

I know I heard him, and I hoped the other girls were taking in what he was saying because I had a lot of undeserved hate coming my way. Sometimes we had gab sessions where we had to go around and spill our guts, and he'd wait for everyone to say something, but this time he was ready to take care of business. No time for emotional girl talk. I didn't have any problems with that.

Just when we were about to go up in the stunt, Jillian said, "Just like you're trying to rob your sister of her boo, don't rob me of my moment and not base right."

I knew my sister heard her; she was the other base. But she didn't even look up. She didn't even get involved. She just let Jillian talk to me any kind of way, and as soon as Jillian went up and put her weight unevenly on me, she came down. I didn't have enough time to get out of the way. She fell directly on my right foot and ankle, and I started screaming in pain.

At first no one rushed up to me—not one girl. Finally, after I cried out, the two coaches came my way, but still the girls stayed back. Thankfully, Coach Pat was an athletic trainer as well as a coach. He tried to calm me down.

"It's not even broken," Coach Pat said after examining it. "It just looks like a little sprain. I'm going to have you sit out for the rest of practice. I'll have one of the alternates take your spot."

The rest of the team went on with practice. Seeing that none of my girls cared that I was injured really got to me. Feeling the pain of the sprain, I just put my head in my hands and sobbed.

"There's nothing wrong with her," Vanessa said rudely to my mom as she came flying into the gym.

"I'm okay, Mom. I'm okay," I said, though it really did hurt.

"I got a text from Coach that you sprained your ankle at practice. I got here as soon as I could. Let's get you to the doctor."

"She needs to go to the doctor, but not for that," my sister said under her breath.

I wanted to get up and punch her, just have an all-out beat down. I mean, how much did she expect me to continue taking? She was acting like a bully, getting all our friends on her side.

My mom hugged me tight, breaking up the tension. I put my arm around her neck, and she helped me hobble to the car. All the while, I continued to receive disheartening sneers and stares from my fellow cheerleaders.

I wanted to talk to each of them individually and let them have it. Skylar needed to be reminded that when she first moved here and needed allies, I was there for her and made sure she knew the routines. When her little sister was abducted, I was worried sick. As for Ariel, she was completely broken-hearted when her uncle was shot to death and his wife, her aunt, was accused of killing him. I was by her side through it all. I believed her aunt was innocent until proven guilty, and that's the way it turned out. And when Yaris first came to Grovehill, the school wasn't as diverse then. Many stayed away from her because of her ethnicity, but I never made her feel anything but welcome.

It was one thing to believe my sister over me, but it was something else all together for me to be physically hurt and for all of them to act like it didn't matter. When I needed them, they were going to stay away? What kind of friends were they? Obviously not mine at all. When my mom pulled into the drug store to get some Icy Hot and a wrap for my leg, I had to stay in the car with Vanessa. She turned around to make a smart comment, and I gave her a look like, *If you say anything to me, you'll regret it.*

"You act like I did this or something, Victoria. We got issues because you crossed the line."

"We got issues because you're a jerk. So high and mighty, thinking you know everything, going behind my back talking about me to everyone. How dare you?" I boldly countered her.

"How dare I? What? Girl, please. Texting my man, stalking him, waiting for him after class, are you serious about that? Like I shouldn't be mad. And people saw you."

"What is it with you, Vanessa? You hate me or something? I told you there's nothing going on between Emerson and me, but you won't let it go. And you're trying to make other people hate me too. I just don't understand you."

"When you get a man and your sister tries to take him away from you, see how you like it. I should've known when you said you wanted us to be friends and you wanted us to be all tight and stuff that it wasn't true. You were jealous of me when your mom started talking to me and hanging out with me more. You were jealous of me when we went down to our grandma's house and she and I had more of a connection because I've spent more time with her. And I should've known you're jealous of me because I have a boyfriend and you don't. I just didn't want to believe it."

"Okay, you might have been right about you and my mom, but I got over it, I apologized for it, and I understood it. And I was never jealous about you and Grandma. I'm just disappointed that it seems like she hates me. But if her granddaughter feels the same way, there's no telling what you told her to make her feel that way about me."

"What are you talking about? I never made you not call her. I know you spend time with your white grandmother. You call her up and say hi."

"Yeah, because she reached out and tried to have a relationship with me over the years. It's not one grandma over the other, and it's definitely not black or white. It's the fact that …" I trailed off, unable to find the right way to explain.

"That what? You can't even come up with some excuse as to why you're not close with your grandmother."

"Because I was a kid, and my grandmother should've reached out to me, okay?"

"Right, and I understand that part of it. But this isn't about that. How do you think I felt being in class, holding my man's phone, and seeing texts from some chick who happens to be my sister trying to get some time with him offline? Your name is not even in his phone. If I didn't know your number, I wouldn't have even known who it was."

"You're reading too much into it."

"Okay, I'm right here. Tell me what's up.

Why were you texting him? Tell me what it was all about."

I just wanted Emerson to give me some advice. I wanted to share with him what was going on with my mom so that he could hopefully help me see that I was reading too much into it. But I couldn't tell Vanessa that until I had all the facts. She couldn't know that I felt my mom was having an affair. She used to detest my mother, and they'd only been cool for a couple of days. If she knew what I thought I knew, for sure, it would be a mess, and I just couldn't chance it. So, it was just better to let my sister keep on taking her anger out on me.

"Just whatever. Believe whatever you want."

"Fine."

"Great."

"I know. Fine. I hate you, and I never want to see you again," Vanessa said to me.

"Don't leave! Don't go! You can't move back to Twiggs County!" I said as I grabbed her shoulder, but she opened up the front door and tried to shrug me off.

"Get off me, Victoria. I'm not going to stay."

"But I need you. I love you."

"Toto, get her!" Vanessa said as a big, rabid dog ran toward my face.

"Oh my gosh, oh my gosh," I uttered. I had to be dreaming. And I was. As soon as the dog bit me, I woke up in a cold sweat.

I had had a nightmare. I got up to go get some water, but my ankle was still hurting, so I took my time. I never made it to the kitchen because as I hobbled past my parents' bedroom I heard noises coming from inside. My mom was giggling and laughing.

When I opened the door, I saw my mom lying stomach-down on the bed talking on her phone. She had rollers in her hair and baggy flannel pajamas on, but she was saying, "Can you visualize me in my lingerie? I'm ready to rock your world. Oh, Ben, tell me more."

Who in the world was Ben? My dad's name was Victor.

"Mom!" I screamed out.

She immediately hung up the phone and came over to me.

"How long were you standing there? I told you to knock on my door before you enter."

"You're the one who had it unlocked! Who

were you talking to? What is all this sex talk, Mom? I want a real explanation," I demanded.

"Calm down, Victoria. It's not what you think."

"Where is Dad?"

"He's on the road at a consulting gig. We're working things out. I told you that."

"You're working things out, but you're talking to some other man on the phone?"

"Okay, let me explain. I'm working a part-time job to help make ends meet."

"I don't understand. Are you hooking up with your new boss or something?" I said, embarrassed to ask my own mother such a question.

She couldn't even look at me.

"I'm sort of like a telemarketer. I never have to meet anybody."

"You mean you're a phone sex operator? Oh my gosh, Mom! No! That's so gross. Really?"

I was appalled. She tried to hug me and tell me it was no big deal, but I backed away, completely irritated and deeply hurt.

CHAPTER FIVE
Powerful Storm

It was seven in the morning, and I hadn't been able to sleep. All night I'd just been staring at the walls, the clock, and the moon, wishing I'd been dreaming hours earlier when I confronted my mom about her racy phone calls. I was more shocked to find out it wasn't what I thought at all. I guess it was a good thing that there was no other man, but how could I consider her selling out like that positive?

Okay, she was making extra income. I remembered hearing my dad complain about being the only breadwinner in the home. My mom had been out of the workforce for years and felt her options were limited. Before I went to bed the night before, she tried explaining that, on paper, if one were to look at her résumé, there weren't a lot of things she could do. She had no references, and her past job experience was from ages ago. One of the mothers on my brother's basketball team had hipped her to her current career path when my mom had confided in her about needing money.

She begged me to keep it under wraps. She said the calls were just a type of acting. While I told her I couldn't keep any promises, I knew deep down I could never sell out my mom. But also I had no peace having to keep all this information locked inside. It was tough. It was like I had elements of the perfect storm brewing around me. Crazy raging winds of turmoil and doubt, bolts of lightning of what would happen if my father found out about this, heated temperatures burning me up because I hated that she felt this was her only option. I needed to escape before this monsoon completely washed me away.

Finally I was able to doze off, but then I awoke to the vibration of my cell phone. It was probably my mom wanting to apologize. Sometimes she called me instead of coming into my room.

When I looked at the number and didn't recognize it, I hesitated. But then curiosity got the better of me, and I cautiously answered the phone. "Hello?"

"Victoria? Are you awake?" a sexy, strangely familiar voice asked.

"It's seven something in the morning. We don't have school. Is this—" I tried asking before I got cut off.

The male said, "I … I'll call back."

"Wait, Stone? Is that you?"

Clearing his throat, his tone confirmed my suspicion. "Yeah, I'm sorry. I just heard last night that you got hurt, and I've been waiting until morning to call and make sure you're okay. Are you?"

"You've been waiting to call me?" I said, in a truly confused voice.

"Yeah, is that okay?"

"That you're calling me?" I clarified.

"I mean, I know it's early," he said.

It was a tad awkward. He really didn't know what to say, and I was still shocked that he called. But Stone had called me to make sure I was okay. Maybe he was a good guy after all.

Then I remembered him talking to Emerson about his dad's concert, so out of the blue I asked, "Are you still planning to go to your dad's concert?"

"I haven't told him I'm coming, but I know he wants me to. I don't know. I really don't feel like driving up there by myself and stuff. I should have gone with him last night if I was going to go."

"I'll go with you," I surprised myself by saying.

"You'll go with me?"

I was suddenly certain that a getaway was just what I needed. I confidently stood by what I'd said. "Yeah, what time do we need to leave? We don't have school, so I can go whenever."

"Well, if you're going to go, I can be there at nine. It will take us about four hours to get down there."

"I'll text you my address."

"Sounds good."

Thankfully my ankle was feeling a little better. Maybe the pain was just in my mind because now that I had somewhere to go, nothing was going to stop me from being ready by nine o'clock. It hadn't even sunk in that I would be going out with Stone. I knew Jillian wanted him, and I got the fact that he wanted her, yet he was coming to pick me up. All the drama and uncertainty was getting annoying.

After I got dressed, I knocked on my mom's door. "Mom, can I come in?"

"Yeah, sweetie, please. Are you okay?" she said as she raised herself up in the bed and rubbed her eyes.

"I'm fine."

"You sure? You have a bunch going on: your ankle, you being upset with me, you not feeling good lately ... I know there's a lot going on with you, Victoria, and I don't want you to think that I don't care. I've been wrestling with it all night hoping you'd understand. I'm hoping that you're okay."

"I'm all right, Mom. I just want to enjoy the day. My friend Stone, you know the one whose dad is—"

"Yeah, in my favorite band, Sweet Lips!"

"Exactly. His dad has a concert early this afternoon."

"I follow them, Victoria. The concert is in Savannah."

"I know. Stone's got his license, and he's going to drive us. We're going to be safe. We'll come right back after the concert's over."

"I don't know."

"Mom, please."

"I don't have any money, honey."

"I still have my money. Dad used to always give us some, and I could never spend it all."

"Right, we need to open you up a bank account."

"I'm taking three hundred dollars. I probably won't spend it all. I'm fine. The concert is early, and we're turning right around after."

"Okay, keep your phone on and call me when you get down there so I can speak to his dad and thank him for having you."

"Okay, I will."

Without me having to be anxious, Stone actually came early. He helped me put my duffel bag in the car. Inside were my cute clothes for the concert since I didn't want to mess them up on the long ride down there, as well as a few toiletries I'd brought, just in case. We were going far away, and you never know what might happen. My mom always taught me that it's better to have it and not need it, than to need it and not have it.

As soon as we got in the car, Stone broke the ice and said, "I'm glad you wanted to do this. I needed to get away."

I smiled. "I'm glad you said yes 'cause I need to get away too."

"Why don't you take your shoe off and put this on your ankle." He reached in the back seat and pulled out an ice bag. "I had one in my freezer from football. You should probably keep it elevated as well. Put it on the dashboard."

"Oh, so you're my nurse?" I teased, actually quite pleased that he cared about my well-being.

"Why can't I be the doctor? You don't think I'm soft, do you?" he said in an alluring voice that threatened to reel me in, but I wasn't going to let him.

"I bet Jillian's going to have a fit if she ever finds out you picked me up."

"And I care why?" he said boldly, clearly serious that he didn't care.

I was confused. Had I imagined he had feelings for her? Certainly not.

Being real, I said, "You know why; you like her."

"No," he said as he looked my way with a coy grin. "I like this beautiful girl who keeps giving me a hard time. Always has something smart to say when I try to reach out. But some of her sassiness is what I like. I just wish she liked me back," he said as he took one finger and gently rubbed the edge of my cheek.

Just his touch set me on fire. This trip wasn't supposed to be about us, but each mile we drove, we connected even more. As we laughed about silly things, we bonded with each other. His dad's new song came on the radio at one point. When I said I liked it, we both reached to turn it up at the same time, and our hands connected. Yeah, something strong was brewing between us. We both felt it. We both knew it. We both liked it.

"Well, we're here." Stone said, not knowing how to respond to the intensity between us.

"Yeah, we better find your dad, huh?" I said as we got out of the car and stepped into the lovely five-star hotel off the river.

"Yeah, I need to get the passes for the concert before he leaves to go over there," Stone replied.

"So you don't need to go to the front desk or anything to find out where he is?"

"No, he always texts me his information."

"You don't think we should call or anything like that in case—"

"What? In case he's getting high or something before the concert?"

Shocked, I said, "No, no, no, I'm not saying that. It's just that most rock stars—"

"What?" Stone asked, cutting me off. "Most rock stars do things to pump themselves up. What's wrong with a little performance enhancement?"

"You condone the fact that your dad—"

"I didn't say my dad was on anything," he said, quickly cutting me off and almost biting my head off at the same time.

I saw that the question hit way too close to home, and since I couldn't figure out how Stone felt about his dad's possible drug use, I dropped it. Besides, I had drama with my mom that I wasn't proud of. I couldn't expect Stone to just trust me right away.

My willingness to let the subject go seemed to take Stone off the defensive.

"Before we go up and see my dad, do you want to go get something to eat?" he asked in a concerned tone, referring to the fact that I hadn't eaten anything all day.

"Nah, I'm fine. Thanks, though," I said, wanting him to drop it. "I had a big breakfast before you picked me up."

"Yeah, but I stopped and got lunch and a snack at the gas station, and you wouldn't get anything."

"I said I'm fine, okay?" I answered, now snapping at him.

Though we'd shared a lot on the ride down— our favorite foods, favorite TV shows, favorite color, and other general stuff—there were some things about me that I'd purposely left out. It actually seemed like he had left some things about himself out as well. I wasn't trying to push him because I didn't want him to push me.

When we got up to the penthouse suite, a large, robust gentleman who must have been the bodyguard opened up the door and grimaced at us until he recognized Stone. I guess he thought I was a groupie or something. His frown was truly scary.

"What's up, man?" he said, loosening up as he gave Stone dap.

"Hey, Thorne." As they interacted I could tell they had a bond.

"Your dad didn't tell me you were coming up."

"Thorne, who's at the door?" I heard a man's voice ask from within the room.

"Lars, sir, it's your son."

"No, it's not. He's at home," Lars replied as both Thorne and Stone shook their heads.

Thorne stepped out of the way and let Stone walk in. When I tried to follow, the buff man resumed his place in the doorway and held up one finger. Why he couldn't open up his mouth and say, "Give them some privacy," "One moment please," or "They need a second," I had no idea. However, I clearly got the message and did not move another muscle, standing stiff like a first grader in time out.

Stone came back to the door and said, "Hey, what are you doing? Let her in. She's with me."

Thorne would not move. So I said, "Go see your dad. I'll just wait right here."

"Clear it with him," Thorne said.

I started to say, "I told you that's what you should have done in the first place," but then thought better of it. When Stone realized I was okay, he walked in to see his father.

"Where are your clothes?" I heard him yell a moment later, sounding totally caught off guard.

And that's when I realized why Thorne wouldn't let me in. Stone's dad was nude, in the middle of the day. But it *was* his hotel room. Maybe his ritual wasn't doing drugs. Or maybe he'd already taken them, and that's why he was walking around in his birthday suit.

"Don't ask me the questions, son. Why are you here? I tried to get you to ride down with me last night. You said, 'No, no, no, I'm just going to rest tomorrow. We have the day off from football. I don't want to do anything.' And then you drive all the way down here on your own. And did I hear a female voice outside? Do you have a girl with you?"

"Shh!" Stone tried getting his dad to calm down, and I could tell he was embarrassed.

"Don't shush me, son. Do her parents know where she is?"

"Yeah, Dad. Her mom wanted to thank you for allowing her to come."

"Well, call her in here. I want to talk to her mom on the phone."

"Put on a robe first!"

"Of course I'm going to put on a robe first!"

When Stone came back to the door, I tried to act like I hadn't heard anything. "I can go down to the lobby and wait," I offered.

"It's cool. Come on in."

The big, muscular giant moved out of the way. He looked me up and down though. I didn't know if I passed whatever test he was giving me, so I just nodded in thanks and followed Stone inside.

"Dad, this is my friend Victoria. Victoria, my father, Lars."

I didn't want to look at him because I was afraid he still didn't have any clothes on. When I peered up, however, I saw he had indeed put on a robe—the manliest, most pretty velvet, purple, and gold robe I'd ever seen. I just wanted to reach out and touch it, but of course I kept my cool.

"My son says that your mom is okay with you being here."

"Yes, sir. I'll call her real quick. I know she wanted to speak to you."

"Yes, let's call her up."

When the phone rang for the fourth time, I was getting nervous. I hoped my mom wasn't on the other line working. She had to answer.

Finally she picked up and said, "Hello?"

"Mom, it's me. I just wanted to let you know I got here okay. I'm here with Stone and his dad."

"Oh, yay! Let me speak to him!" she said, all excited.

Because I was standing in front of Mr. Bush, I couldn't tell my mom to calm down, and I didn't have to because he could hear her excitement through the phone. He must have been used to that, though. He took the phone from me, and after he and my mom exchanged a few pleasantries, he asked whether my being there was okay with her. Seeming satisfied with her response, he said good-bye and handed the phone back to me.

As soon as Mr. Bush was done talking to my mom, the entourage that usually accompanies a rock star began showing up. Makeup artists, wardrobe people, and fans with VIP access came in and flocked around Stone's dad. Then a logistics team came in, putting a damper on the party.

"A storm is supposed to come through here tonight around midnight," a serious-looking lady from the team informed Mr. Bush. "I'm only telling you because storms are unpredictable, and it could come earlier. It's not even supposed to hit this particular area badly, but that could always change. We're just checking because we wanted you to be aware in the event that you want to cancel."

"No, no, no, we can't cancel," a shady-looking man interjected. "This show's been sold out for months. I've been checking the weather, and it's under control. I didn't even want to bother you with this. We're going to be fine."

But I could see the look of concern on Mr. Bush's face. However, the man, who must've been some sort of concert promoter, kept reassuring him about the storm and pushing him to do the show. Finally, Mr. Bush conceded and agreed to go on as planned. The concert promoter ushered him out of the room to meet with the other band members before the show, and the entourage followed them out.

As everyone cleared out, Stone and I went from being surrounded by a million people to being the only two in the room. We were staring at each other face to face.

"How could you not be intrigued by all this?" I asked. He'd looked annoyed and somewhat bored by all the hubbub before.

"I'm intrigued by you," he replied. He brushed my face with the back of his hand so gently that I melted like chocolate left out in the hot sun.

"Why did you tell me that you liked me earlier?"

"Because I do."

"No, you don't. You've been looking at Jillian and other girls. Not at me."

"Then I'll have to show you that I like you, since you don't believe what I'm saying."

Stone leaned down and kissed me, slowly, affectionately, and passionately. Everything on the inside of me was squirming as I kissed him back. I didn't know what I was doing, but I had no problem figuring it out because having our lips intertwined seemed as natural as a baby sucking a bottle. No one told me how to do it. Some things you just instinctively know. He took one hand and put it around my waist; the other hand he put on my back.

I moaned, and he asked, "Am I hurting you?"

"No, I just ..." I turned away, too embarrassed to say that I didn't know passion felt that good. "I've never done anything like this," I mumbled instead.

"Let me be your guide."

And when he kissed me again, I felt like I was being lifted up off of my feet by a tornado. But I wasn't scared—quite the contrary. I loved being swept away.

Despite the storm warning, Sweet Lips decided to have the concert. I felt so thrilled to be around Stone, yet so uncomfortable at the same time. We needed to get to the concert. We rode over in the limousine with his dad. His father seemed like he was in the zone; he was leaning back against the seat listening to music with his earphones in. It sort of felt like he was barely aware we were there. I could sense Stone's frustration. If his dad did this to him all the time, I could understand why there was distance between them. Nonetheless, he said he was excited we were there. I was having the time of my life hanging out with a real rock star.

When we got to the concert venue, we went into the green room with Mr. Bush, and there were all types of goodies. Sweet Lips was the headliner, so there were other acts already playing on stage. Each group decided to do one less song so that if the storm changed course and got nasty, the concert would be done in plenty of time to get people out safely.

"You keep staring at me," I said to Stone as we followed Thorne to a place near the front of the stage.

"I can't help it. I like what I see."

"You're not too bad to look at yourself. But we're here to watch your father."

"I've seen this show I don't know how many times. And after every performance, my dad comes home and wants me to check out the video, as if it differs."

"So if you've seen his band so many times, why are we here?"

"Because you said you'd come with me. I didn't want to give up a chance to get to know you more. It's fate. We're supposed to be here at this exact moment."

He put his hands around my waist and pulled me to him. He'd been taking real good care of me, making sure I ate a little. He didn't even know I had an eating disorder. He just wouldn't let me starve. He was around me every second, so I couldn't throw it up. So I ate in moderation. Honestly, I think my stomach appreciated being able to keep something down. We didn't go out there until his dad was about to go on because Stone didn't want me standing up for too long. With all the excitement between the two of us, I'd actually forgotten that I'd hurt my ankle.

"Ladies and gentlemen!" the announcer came on and said. "Are you ready to have your breath taken away? To see a show like you've never seen before? To be lifted to another place in space? If you are, get on your feet and make some noise for Sweet Lips!"

People started screaming and chanting for the band, and I joined in because, for the first time in a long time, I was happy. I felt beautiful, and I felt free.

"Thank you so much for bringing me!" I yelled loud enough for Stone to hear me.

And I took both of my hands and wrapped them around his so he could squeeze me tighter. He nibbled on my ear a little, and I melted even more. I leaned my head back on his chest.

"You okay?" he asked.

"Perfect," I said to him.

"My dad better come on out here and get this concert started."

"Yeah, look at the flaps on the top of the stage. They're blowing mighty hard."

Suddenly a big crack of thunder rocked the arena, followed by two intense bolts of lightning. The stage started to shake intensely. The screams of excitement turned to screams of terror as the right side of the stage came down. Then pandemonium broke out.

"Oh my gosh, Stone! Oh my goodness!"

"Just hold on to my hand."

"I can't run that fast! My ankle!"

Then someone screamed out, "I'm stuck, I'm stuck!" We saw a woman trapped under part of the stage.

He let my hand go and went to help the lady. Then the rest of the stage started collapsing too. I couldn't get to him anymore as people began stampeding away from that area, pushing me further from him. I felt like I was getting trampled. I couldn't leave him back there, but I couldn't go against the crowd either.

I kept shouting, "Stone! Stone!"

I didn't hear him respond back. We had to stay together because the wind was pushing us back. I was holding on to people that I'd never met in my life. I was pulling people forward who needed my assistance.

Rain started coming down in sheets; the weather was showing us no mercy. Then there was a siren signaling some crisis. We were all outside. Where could we go to get out of the storm's path? Nowhere. As I was running to go up the hill where the wind didn't seem to be blowing as hard a few feet away, I came across a man who was on the ground. His face was bloody. I reached down and pulled him up. He just held on to me and squeezed me tight, crying in my arms.

"You don't know how many people passed by me. You don't know how many people wouldn't stop. No one cared. You saved me. Over and over they were stomping on my face. No one would help. They only cared about themselves, but you saved me. Thank you! My wife was near the stage. I couldn't get there. I think she's gone," said the bald-headed gentleman, who looked to be in his thirties.

That's when I realized that Stone might be gone too. I screamed so loud that it hurt, but the man wouldn't let me stay there. He kept pushing me out of harm's way. As the rain dropping from the sky turned to hail, I hoped that we only had a few seconds left in this horrible, powerful storm.

CHAPTER SIX

Open Heart

I was a base for cheerleading, and I needed to summon that strength so I could help this wounded man. The strong winds were beginning to pick up debris from the collapsed stage and hurl it around. I needed to get him to safety. Help was needed all around us, but people were frantically running all about, only concerned with saving themselves. As bad as I wanted to find Stone, it was too dangerous to turn back. And this man I didn't even know was counting on me to help him first.

"Come on, sir. Stay up. You can do it!"

"Just leave me. If my wife is gone, I don't want to live."

"No, sir. Come on. Come on! She's okay. I know somebody else has probably got her. I've got to get you to safety! Come on!" I said, knowing I wouldn't be able to live with myself if I didn't do all I could to make sure he survived.

The debris was really flying now. We had to move faster. Someone running right beside me was taken down by a flying trash can. With all the strength inside me, I put the gentleman's arm around my neck, and we took off. I saw bloody noses and cut arms and legs. I heard squeals. Louder than any of that, I heard the roar of the storm.

Everyone was running to a nearby hangar. People there were helping usher the concertgoers safely inside. At the front of the hangar door was Stone's dad, Lars. He was making sure everyone was okay. People smiled when they saw the lead singer of Sweet Lips was out there to help them.

As I helped the man get to safety inside the hangar, I saw his face change and light up. "Pamela!" he screamed. And he ran up to a woman who I assumed was his wife.

Just then, Mr. Bush caught sight of me and asked where Stone was. I yelled out, "I don't know, but he was helping a woman when the stage collapsed. I think he's trapped underneath. I tried to go back. I couldn't … I couldn't."

"Thorne! Let's go get my son," Lars said with a look of desperation plastered across his face.

"I gotta come with you," I begged.

He placed his hands on my shoulders and uttered, "No, my son told me your ankle is already hurt. Thankfully you've helped this gentleman, and there are others here that need help too. Besides it's still too dangerous out there."

"The storm is passing," I argued, needing to help find the one that had entered my heart.

"But it hasn't passed completely yet." Lars pointed toward the blowing winds.

I nodded, surely not wanting to get in the way. Stone's father and Thorne, along with a bunch of other men, took off. I watched them until a little red-haired girl tugged on my sweater.

She was crying, "I don't know where my mommy is! My mommy got taken by the wind."

The little girl had to be no more than six. Watching her tears flow, I felt my heart sink lower than a submarine combing the bottom of the sea. I lifted her into my arms and held her tight.

"It's okay. It's going to be all right."

She was desperate to find her mommy, and I was desperate to find Stone, so we searched the hangar. Maybe someone missed him. As soon as I found a guy who liked me, who made me smile, who made me feel special, who made me feel on top of the world, my world got turned upside down. I felt just like the little girl who needed her mom.

I had needed to talk to mine to let her know how much I loved her. I hadn't been outright mean when we left, but I was sort of cold and real judgmental about her lifestyle and what she was doing. She was just trying to take care of our family, and I needed to believe her. I knew she loved my dad. Why was I second-guessing that?

Nobody's cell phones were working now. My ankle started hurting. I went toward the front of the hangar, sat down on the concrete with the little girl on my lap, and just rocked her back and forth. I felt like I was in hell. The screams of agony coming from people in their own physical pain, or the pain of wondering where a loved one was, were almost too much to bear.

Just when I thought there was no hope, the little girl's mom ran up and said, "Emily!"

Everyone around me started crying tears of joy. Emily needed her mom, and she found her mom. If that could happen, anything was possible.

Stone's dad returned with his search party. They all looked battered from the elements. Frantically, I searched their faces. I didn't see Stone among them, only a person covered in mud. Then I realized who it was.

I ran over to them and threw myself on Stone, hugging him as tightly as I could. He was a little gritty, sporting mud all over, but he was in one piece.

"I thought you were gone," I kept repeating.

"No, I'm okay. I tried to help as many people as I could, and I got trapped. But I'm okay."

Tears streamed from my eyes. I was over-whelmed with joy. Stone was okay after all. I didn't want that moment to end. I didn't want to let him out of my sight for the fear that I might lose him again.

Lars's entourage surrounded him. The manager didn't want him making any statements suggesting that any of this was his fault. I knew it was eating Lars up that he didn't heed the given warning and cancel the concert.

The fire trucks were pulling up near the collapsed stage and the hangar, one after another. More sirens followed as ambulances and police cars came too. This was a living nightmare.

The storm finally passed, but the damage it had left was worse than anything I'd ever seen. The worst was where the stage had come down. Stone's father couldn't babysit us because this was a PR nightmare for his group.

We stayed another hour or two, helping everyone we could get to safety, find loved ones, or deal with the grief. It was confirmed that there were nine fatalities. When we got in the car to head back to the hotel, Stone's dad had me call my mom and put him on the phone. I could hear her screaming hysterically. However, I could tell she calmed down some when he told her that I was okay.

He asked if it was okay that I stay with him and Stone overnight, and he said he would make sure that I got back home safely. When he put me on the phone she was crying uncontrollably.

"I heard about what happened at the concert. I called you, but I couldn't get through. Oh, Victoria, I love you, sweetie!"

"I love you too, Mom. Sorry about earlier."

"I know. I trust you."

"I'm okay. We're okay."

"You be good tonight, okay?"

"Yes, ma'am."

We were in the suite, and I was nestled in Stone's arms.

"I can't believe everything that happened tonight," he said.

I wanted to hear about his ordeal. I could only imagine how horrible it must have been to be pinned down by the stage, but he didn't want to talk about it, so I didn't push. The important thing was that he was okay. A little shaken, but alive.

"Nine people lost their lives, Victoria."

"I know," I said to him. "It could have been many more if you didn't help."

He nodded.

Earlier we thought we had come down to this concert to connect with each other. Now we had more clarity. The bigger reason was so that we could be in place to connect with those in need.

"You just don't know how bad I need you right now," Stone said to me as he looked deep into my eyes.

I could tell he just wanted to devour me like I was Thanksgiving dinner or something. Like a well-behaved vampire resisting blood, I was able to keep myself away from him. However, we'd just gone through so much. We needed to deal with the truth. When he leaned in to kiss me, I pulled back.

"What's wrong? You know you want me. I can tell you're feeling me. My dad even told me how upset you were when I—"

"Yes," I said as I put my index finger over his lips so that he couldn't speak. Now it was my turn.

I'd gone through a near-death experience, and I couldn't be passive anymore. I had issues. There was no point in adding more problems to my plight.

"I'm so broken, Stone."

"What do you mean? You broke your leg?

Your ankle? I knew you shouldn't have been out there with your injury."

"No, no, I didn't mean physically broken," I hurried to assure him. "Metaphorically, I'm all messed up on the inside, and I don't think it would be fair to you. Taking this to another level without you truly knowing what you're about to get involved with wouldn't be right. If you knew the whole truth, you would run to the elevator and press the lobby button so hard—"

"Okay, okay. You're being dramatic. What are you talking about? No one is perfect. I'm surely not."

"Exactly. I know you got some things going on too that you haven't shared with me. I want to be here for you. I don't want to be someone you have a good time with and don't talk to the next day."

"Oh, is that what you think this is to me?"

"I don't know. We haven't talked about it. All of this is brand new, and already you want to get between the sheets. You don't even know what's in my head." I looked away.

Stone gently brought my face back to him. "I find that a little strange for you to say. I've known you for so long, Victoria. You have sensed my interest, and I've picked up vibes from you feeling me too. Or at least I thought so."

"You know my name, but you don't know my issues. You've flirted, but you haven't felt my pain. I want a boyfriend who can help me through my real pain. I don't want someone to be so naive to his own woes that he doesn't want to talk about them to me," I said as I paused, thinking about my state of mind. "Honestly, right now I'm so weak that I couldn't help you with your problems if you did share them, you know? You and I have to get stronger. We've got a new opportunity, a new chance at life. We can't blow it."

I took a real chance saying all that to Stone. We'd had a big night. He was trying to salvage it and make the night better for both of us. Since we were already raw, I wanted things to get even more emotionally intense. I was waiting for him to rise up at any moment and bail on me, but he didn't. He grabbed my hand, stroked it gently, touched my face lightly, looked like he was making love to me with his brown eyes, and said, "When the stage came down on me, I thought about you and how sad I was that I wasn't going to get to fully know you. Admittedly, I'm a guy whose mind does stay on one thing, but listening to you now, I think it's much deeper. I have lots of issues too, and to know that you care enough to want to get to know me more in spite of my issues means so much."

Jerking back my hand, I said, "I can't take the way you're looking at me, Stone, because I hate my body. All right?"

"What do you mean? You're gorgeous."

"You're just saying that," I said as I stood up from the couch and walked toward the window.

"No, I've been watching you, and I mean it." He got up too and came to stand with me. "I love your body." He placed his frisky hands around my waist and pulled me to him.

Hearing him say that he thought I was fine meant a lot. Regrettably, I was unable to see myself the same way. I sighed.

"What else is going on with you, Victoria? There is more going on than just you not liking your body. I can tell."

Without holding back, I let him truly in. "I've been practicing some unhealthy eating habits. I won't eat at all some days, or I'll eat so much, and then when no one's looking, I'll throw it up."

"Are you serious?" he said as he stroked my back. "Why? You look amazing. You're thin and gorgeous."

I was relieved that I hadn't scared him away. He was there, right there—truly with me.

"I hate myself when I do those things. I know it's unhealthy, and I know it's not right, and I don't think I'm bulimic or anything like that because this is all new. It started a few days ago. But if I don't fix this, if I don't get a hold of this unhealthy way, it's going to ruin me. I can't be in a relationship if I'm messed up. You know?"

"Yeah, I do."

"But you don't know. You're so perfect and together."

"No, I *know*." The serious way he said those three words pulled on my heart. "Coach was threatening to take my spot away early in the season. Then there's this sophomore who's a natural athlete, and honestly he should be playing."

"But you do so great when you're out there."

He shook his head. "I've dropped a couple passes, and it's been hard, and so I'm the opposite. You want to get your body smaller—which is ridiculous, by the way, because you are already too small—and I want to get my muscles bigger. So—"

"So what?" I said, needing him to open up and trust me too.

"I've been taking some steroid pills. I tried not to go over-the-top. I gotta stop because the side effects are killing me. And living through tonight, I want to be better."

"Wow, me too," I said, moving closer to him.

Because he'd trusted me to listen and not judge, I definitely needed to do the same, and I did really understand. The pressures of being a teenager were overwhelming. We both had jobs. I needed to be a cute, energetic cheerleader, and he needed to be the strong, perfect football player. Our bodies needed to comply with those expectations, and when they weren't doing it on their own, we sought out extra measures to make sure it happened—talk about hating yourself.

"I thought my life was over. I thought the storm was karma because I'd been doing something illegal, even though this past week was the first time I've taken them. But I did run extra fast in the last game," Stone said.

"Where'd you get them?"

"Thorne. My dad's top bodyguard."

"Yeah, I know who Thorne is," I said, thinking back to how he'd made sure I didn't enter the suite until I was invited.

"If my dad knew, he'd have a fit, and I don't want to take them anymore. They've actually been making me jumpy and aggressive. I've been resenting this life when most kids would be excited to have a dad who's a rock star, you know?"

"Yeah, I do." I resented my dad for being a player back in his day. "My dad used to be on top of the world the way yours is when he was in the NBA, and now he's just trying to hold on. Be excited for your dad that things are good."

"I'm trying to be. I'm excited about you," he said as he kissed me on the cheek. "Maybe now that we've both been vulnerable and let out what's been going on with each other, we can help each other through."

We came even closer. A razor blade would not have been able to get through. Our lips met.

I was so thrilled. Not only the passion, but also the honesty between us made the kiss that much more special.

Our tongues were going at it. His hands were roaming all up my shirt. I felt uneasy and wonderful all at the same time. Just as we were moving the kiss from the window to the couch, there was a pounding on the door. The sound was almost desperate and frightening. We jumped apart.

"Coming!" Stone yelled out.

Since his dad was in a meeting in the conference room of the hotel, no bodyguards were guarding the door. Stone was leery because, though his father didn't control the weather, there had been media reports that people were angry and upset with his band for not canceling. It could have been an enraged fan coming to exact revenge.

"Be careful," I said to him.

"You don't have to worry. I'm not opening that door," Stone said to me. Then he called out a little louder, "Who is it?"

"It's Mr. House, Victoria's father." When I heard it was my dad, I jumped to my feet.

"Please let me in now." He knocked again.

Quickly I fixed my outfit, smoothed my hair, and wiped the lipstick off of my chin. Stone let my dad in. As soon as he saw me, he rushed over to where I was standing.

"Dad, I'm okay," I said in an assuring voice as I hugged him tight.

"Oh my gosh, Victoria, you don't know how worried I was. Get your stuff, sweetie. We're going home."

"But I'm okay. I was planning on coming home tomorrow. Mom already talked to Stone's dad."

"I was finishing up some consulting work in Statesboro when I heard what happened. It wasn't that far of a drive for me to come to Savannah to get you. You're going home tonight." He paused for a minute and seemed to register the situation. "Where is his dad by the way? It's just the two of you guys up here in this suite?"

"He had to go downstairs and help his management and the concert crew," I quickly explained.

"I can call him if you'd like, sir, but your daughter and I were just talking," Stone tried explaining.

My dad frowned his way. "I've been seventeen years old, young man. Try to lie to somebody who's forgotten. That somebody isn't me. I know how hormones rage at your age. You guys did answer the door relatively fast, so I think I caught you before you went too far."

"Dad!" I said, completely embarrassed.

"Whatever. Let's go."

My dad went over to Stone. I did not want to leave. Having no choice, I got out my purse and bag and went toward the door.

"I'll call you," Stone said.

My dad leaned over and said something to him that I could not hear.

"Yes, sir," he quickly replied, and we were gone.

As soon as we got in the elevator, my dad pulled me to him and hugged me again.

"I was so worried. In the middle of a storm like that? Lives lost? My baby girl? What was your mom thinking letting you come down here with this boy?"

The last thing I wanted was for my dad to be angry with my mom. My family needed to heal. My dad needed to hear from me. We needed to have a tough heart to heart. I wasn't trying to be an adult, but I could no longer sit idly by and say nothing.

When we got to the lobby, Stone's dad was waiting by the elevator door to go up. When Lars got a glimpse of me, concern brushed his face. Thorne picked up on it and blocked my dad from me. I realized they didn't know he was my father.

"Is everything okay?" Mr. Bush asked.

"Yes, sir. This is my dad."

"Oh, okay."

Thorne stepped back.

"I appreciate you having my daughter at your concert. She's a big fan, and my wife's a big fan too. You had one tough night."

"Yeah."

"I'm glad you're okay. I'm going to go ahead and get my baby home. I know you have a lot to handle here, and I'll just get her out of the way. Thanks for having her," my dad said, smiling.

Lars smiled back. "Absolutely, absolutely. She was no trouble at all. I made sure she was safe, but I understand you wanting to get her home. I'm glad my son had her."

"What do you mean?" my dad said, almost insulted.

"I mean I'm glad they're friends. She's a truly genuine young lady, with spunk to boot. She helped save a lot of lives tonight, and while I didn't want her in the situation we were thrown in, she was an angel. Because she was here, many others are still here as well. You know what I'm saying?"

"Yeah, I do," my dad said as he reached out to shake Mr. Bush's hand. "Thanks for telling me that." And they shook on it.

"Victoria, thank you. And stay on my son. That is, if your father lets you all be friends after this." He grinned at me, and I smiled back. Stone and I were connected regardless of what my dad thought.

We went out of the hotel. I could see the penthouse window from the parking lot. I could almost feel Stone looking out, not wanting me to go. I didn't want to leave either, but it was okay because we had a bond.

"Call your mom, and let her know I got you."

"No, Dad. I'd like to talk to you first. Please. You came all this way down here to get me. We have time to drive in the car and talk alone. I want to tell you something."

"Okay, we can do that. I'm glad you're okay," he said. "I needed to see for myself. Wasn't gonna leave my baby down here in all this craziness."

"I'm glad I'm okay too, Dad. It was really scary."

"So I hear. That's why you shouldn't have been down here. Anything could have happened. If something had, I would have never been able to forgive your mom."

"But, Dad, she's doing the best she can all alone. You told me y'all worked it out, and y'all were going to be together again, but I don't know. It just seems like y'all aren't back on track."

"It takes time, Victoria."

"I know, but if tonight has taught me anything, it's that time isn't promised. We have to make the best of the time we are given. If there's something you have to say to Mom, it doesn't need to be filled with anger. She is doing the best she can, but she's her best when you're around. I needed to be where I was tonight, Dad. I've been so unhappy, so depressed, so down, so discouraged, so distraught, and seeing my life almost taken away was like being charged by a positive bolt of lightning."

"Did one strike you?"

"No, Dad, though it came close. I think when I saw people falling, bruised, battered, gone, that's when I realized that I didn't want to live my life in such a gloomy way. I want to be respectful of my parents, but if I have something to say to you guys like, 'I love y'all, but I need you to get your acts together,' I want to be able to have that conversation. If I want to say that I need help because I don't feel beautiful and that I'm doing things to myself that are unhealthy, I need to be able to have that conversation with my father so he can tell me that I'm beautiful and that I can get over it."

"You are beautiful, babe."

"I believe that now, Dad."

"What kind of help do you need? What have you been doing to yourself?"

"I've been making myself throw up because I hate my body. I want to talk to my counselor at school. You know, the cheerleading coach's wife?"

"She's your coach too, right?"

"Yeah. I'm going to be okay, but if I hadn't been here tonight during this tragedy, I don't know if I would be."

He touched my shoulder and told me he loved me. When we got home, it was about five in the morning. I had planned on going straight to bed, but my mom and Vanessa were waiting up. They both hugged me so tight, it was crazy. And instead of my dad being mad at my mom, they actually talked. Vanessa and I went into my bedroom and did the same.

My sister said, "Oh my gosh, I thought that you were gone. You go to a concert, and the next thing we hear is there's a crazy storm and people are getting killed. I didn't know if one of those people was you. The last thing I said to you was that I was angry, and I was mad and—"

"You don't have to explain. I understand."

"But you said that you didn't like Emerson, and clearly you don't. You went out of town with Stone. Oh, girl, that was gangsta."

"You're so silly." I couldn't believe I was smiling at Vanessa.

"Why were you trying to text Emerson, though?"

"I just needed his advice." I still could not squeal on my mom.

"Here I was so stupid, acting so jealous that I got in the way of you getting advice. It's crazy. I'm sorry."

"I just want you to know that I love you, Vanessa, and I might make mistakes, but they won't be intentional."

"I love you too. I can't believe I got everybody to be mad at you. I was being an idiot."

Knowing I was no longer going to hold back with people, I said, "In the future, if you ever feel like I'm doing you wrong, talk to me, hear me out, and let me at least explain. I really need my sister, but for us to have a good relationship I need you to have an open heart."

Happy Place

I was so thankful that my mom let me go to school the next day. The last thing I wanted to do was sit around and relive the horror of the storm. Nine lives lost around me; it was devastating. But knowing that there could have been many more had Stone and I not been there to be strong and help people through was uplifting.

I was a little bummed that Stone wouldn't be in school. His dad was still doing damage control and wasn't planning to leave Savannah for at least a few more days. But when my mom dropped Vanessa and me off, I saw handsome Stone Bush walking in the door too.

"Hey, you!" he said, as he gave me a wide smile.

"What are you doing here?" I said, smiling back and wanting to just reach out and hug him tight.

"After you left, I couldn't sleep. My dad had one of his bodyguards drive me back. I came to school because I had to make sure you were okay," he said as he brushed my face with such gentle strokes that I felt warm like he had made me feel the night before.

"Ugh, excuse me, this is not a hotel," Vanessa said, inserting herself between the two of us.

"Vanessa!" I said to my sister as I blushed.

My sister tugged me away. "Excuse us."

"I want to talk to him," I said to her. "I want to see if he's okay."

"Girl, he likes you a lot," my sister explained.

"I know," I said, feeling confident about what we had, which was real.

She continued her inquiry. "What about your eating disorder? I mean, I'm not trying to get in your business or anything, but do you think it's wise to keep secrets and—"

"No, no, no, he knows about it."

"Really? Y'all talked that deeply?"

"Vanessa, you of all people should know that a near-death experience can bring you closer to those who matter in your life."

"Point taken. When I came out of the hospital and had a new chance at living my life, I wanted to make every second count. But boys can sometimes be the opposite. Emerson pulled away from me for a while after those gang members beat him up. However, if Stone came to school to make sure you're all right, obviously that's not the case. Go on and talk to him." She turned back to Stone, who was waiting by the lockers a few steps behind us. "Take care of my sister!"

He was looking at my hand. I could tell he wanted to hold it, but it was awkward, so he said, "I got you!" to Vanessa. She was satisfied and walked on.

"You didn't have to come all the way back up here so soon on my account. You could've stayed with your dad."

"Well, I had to get my car back up here anyway, and then some other stuff came up that made me want to leave. But who am I kidding?

I wanted to see you. I'm glad you came to school because if you wouldn't have been here, I woulda had to figure out some way to check out and head over to your house to see you."

"You wouldn't have done that," I said, completely blushing, as my toes curled from excitement.

We went on to literature class. Before I could get in the door, Skylar, Ariel, and Yaris were waiting for me. He stepped to the side, but waited.

"Oh my gosh, Victoria, you're okay!" Skylar said as she grabbed me tight and squeezed me hard.

"Ouch!" I yelled out.

"I'm just sorry I've been such a jerk to you," she said.

"We all have," Yaris added as she stroked my arm.

"Vanessa called us last night. She was so worried. We were all so worried," Ariel said. "And you're okay?" She looked at my guy. "Stone, why didn't you tell us you liked our girl? I actually thought you liked Jillian. Sorry, Victoria, I'm just being real, and I want to make sure this slick joker is too."

"Ariel, Jillian's not my type," Stone manned up and told her. "She's too controlling, and she thinks she knows it all. Plus, I've got my eye on someone else. We've got class. Bye."

"Ohhh!" all three of them said in unison as Stone put his arm around my shoulder and led me inside our class.

"You haven't made me your girl," I said to him. Then I went to my seat, leaving him at the door to ponder my words.

Ms. Upshaw went up to him, and they stepped back into the hall. She was probably concerned about everything we'd just gone through in Savannah.

Emerson was already seated at his desk. He turned to me and said, "Your sister told me you needed to talk to me about something. Sorry I misjudged. I just was nervous. I didn't know what was going on with you. She said you were texting me, and she was mad, and—"

"I know. I should have just told her what was going on, but it was a lot of personal stuff. I'm good now."

Our teacher and Stone came into the class. She gave a nice speech about the importance of life. Everyone was amazed to learn that Stone and I were actually at the concert tragedy they had heard about on the news. People were happy we were okay.

My eyes met Stone's. We were happy we were okay too. She wanted the class to write a paper about what we were thankful for, and I just became so emotional and so choked up that I ran out of the room. I tried to catch my breath, but it felt like I was suffocating, unable to breathe.

Ms. Upshaw followed me out and said, "Do you need to go get some water?"

"Can I go to see the counselor, please?"

"Yes, just let me write you a pass."

Stone came to the door, but the teacher wouldn't let him near me. "She'll be fine."

When I got to the counselor's office, someone else was already in there. Life as a teenager wasn't easy. It was always something. Many if not all of us at Grovehill had some type of drama we had to live with and soldier through. Thank goodness we had our counselors there to help. Many of us didn't take advantage of it. I was trying not to be impatient because those that did need help needed to receive it, so I sat there and waited.

Ten long minutes passed before Coach Joann came out and called me into her office. On my way in, I passed the other student coming out, and I was surprised to see it was Jillian. Just seeing her getting help made me feel sorry for her.

"What can I do?" Coach Joann asked me when we were settled into her office. "What can I help you with? I've seen your weakness and lack of energy at practice. I know you've been unhappy. What's going on, Victoria?"

"I've been so depressed about my body that I hurt myself physically by not eating enough or making myself throw up when I do eat. I don't want to be so hard on myself about my weight and appearance. I'm still just a kid basically."

"You're right. Do you think you'll be able to stop binging and purging?"

"I'm committed to stopping."

"Do you think you're beautiful? Do you like your body?"

"I'm trying to like it. I was telling my dad the ordeal I went through last night. You know what I went through, right?" She nodded, indicating she'd heard about the concert. "It just made me realize that I want to be able to come to you or my family and friends to talk about stuff. Obviously I still have some issues to work through, and I don't want to be so caged up about them. I don't want to be boxed in. I don't want to be unhappy."

"Well, the first step toward happiness is talking through your problems and realizing every day isn't going to be perfect. It's how you look at the day. It's how you're thankful for what you have. There are a lot of support groups for eating disorders. Here are some pamphlets. When you look in the mirror, I think all you see is imperfection. When I look at you, I see a girl who's strong and healthy."

She held my hand and squeezed it tight. I believed her. Knowing that I needed help and seeking it out wasn't a bad thing at all. I was going to be okay.

Time was flying. It was Friday night. Though we won our away game, it hadn't been great for Stone—he'd been benched. Now we were loading onto the buses to head back to Grovehill.

I wanted to go up to him and say, "You guys

won the game. You'll do better next time. It'll be okay. Don't stress." But he looked like he didn't want to be bothered.

"Are you going to sit with Stone on the bus?" Vanessa asked as Emerson was waiting for her.

Skylar was sitting by Ford, Yaris was beside Hagen, and Ariel and Ryder were paired up. But Stone didn't get on the bus with all of my friends. He got on the first bus that was for football players only. That was my clue that he wasn't trying to hang out with me, and I wasn't trying to push it. The crew could be a little overwhelming, and I could tell he was getting teased because of his performance.

"I don't think so," I answered Vanessa. I got on the bus, put on my headphones, and leaned back against the seat.

I was happy that I cared about Stone, and I wasn't trying to read too much into the fact that he wasn't feeling me at the time. People needed their space to breathe and deal with some stuff on their own, and while I wanted to be there for him, I wasn't him, and I was okay with that. I was really proud of myself for being in such a healthy place. Just when I had become excited about my space, not being all bummed out about what I didn't have, someone touched my shoulder. I opened my eyes and saw it was Stone.

"Anybody sitting here?"

"No, but I thought you were on the—"

"I was but ... but I could use some company instead of wallowing. Cool?"

"Sure," I said, moving my pompoms and allowing him to sit down.

"I'm struggling, Victoria. I can't let my spot be taken indefinitely."

"Everybody can have a bad game."

"It's just ... I don't feel the same way I did last week."

"Last week you were on steroids."

"Shhh!" he abruptly hushed me as he looked around, making sure no one was paying any attention to us.

"I wouldn't rat you out. I'm just saying that you moved on from all that. You've just got to find a way to tap into your strength without drugs to help, and you know I'm saying this from the bottom of my heart. I mean, I'm there with you. I still struggle too, but I'm overcoming. You helped get me there. What we went through, you made sure I was there. Don't let difficult circumstances dictate poor choices."

"You sound like a parent," he snapped at me abruptly, clearly upset.

Trying to get to the bottom of his mood, I said, "So what's been up with you?"

"What? Is it bad that I haven't called you the last couple days? Heck, when I saw you Wednesday in school, we were cool. You expect me to call every day? Yesterday we had a double practice, and I had to get ready for the game."

"I was just asking. I'm fine, and no, I don't expect anything from you. I was clear you haven't made me your girlfriend. I'm not trying to be high maintenance. I just want to make sure you're okay. Something else seems to be weighing on you."

"My mom called," he barely got the words out.

"That's a great thing!"

"You know what? You don't understand. Maybe I shouldn't have sat here. Maybe it wasn't a good idea," he angrily said, getting up before the buses even took off.

I don't know if he thought I was gonna stop him or what, but I was in a good place. I had to stop letting what other people thought affect how I felt. If I couldn't be myself around this guy, it was good to know it now before my feelings got even deeper. I was already thinking about him morning, noon, and night. Maybe it was time for a break. I saw Emerson get up and follow him out.

My sister came back three seats to where I was sitting and sat beside me. "What's up Stone's butt?" she bluntly asked me.

"Who knows?" I replied. We both chuckled.

Vanessa stopped laughing and said, "No, seriously, Victoria. Are you okay?"

"Yeah, if I can't be me around him, I don't want to be with him."

"I know—that's right," she lifted her hand for dap, and I obliged.

She put her arm through mine, and I rested my head on her shoulder. She might have thought I was upset, and I didn't protest her wanting to take care of me because I was a little sleepy. I truly appreciated that she cared.

When we got to the school, Stone was the first one all up in my face. "I'm sorry. I just needed to cool down. You made a positive comment about my mom, and it's such a sore subject with me. I didn't mean to pout and stomp off like a baby." I just shrugged my shoulders and started walking off. He caught up and kept talking. "Wait, wait, can I make it up to you? I know you're hungry. Can we go out? Talk?"

"I'm riding home with Skylar, but thanks. My mom's expecting me."

"Please, Victoria. Please give me another chance. We should slide by Waffle House to chat for a bit. I'll have you home in no time. Promise."

He continued begging and being pitiful. I held up one finger, signaling for him to wait. With my other hand, I reached in the pocket of my letterman's jacket and pulled out my cell phone to call my mom.

She said, "Hey, honey! I saw you guys won."

"Yes, ma'am. We made it back to the school."

"Well, I thought your sister was coming home with Skylar, but now it looks like she has other plans."

"I was calling for sort of the same reason."

"I suspected as much."

"Stone wants to take me to dinner, so I'll be home a little later. Is that okay?"

"Just be in by eleven thirty."

"Mom, that's only an hour away."

"If that doesn't work, then you better get Skylar to bring you home now."

"Yes, ma'am," I said.

Stone and I said nothing in the car on the way to Waffle House. I don't know if we both were looking forward to the signature meal, or if it was still sort of awkward between us, and neither of us knew how to bridge the gap. However, like a prosecuting attorney, he had the burden of proof. If he wanted another chance, he needed to earn it. Besides, he's the one who wanted to spend time with me.

We pulled into the parking lot. I turned to open the door, but before I could reach the handle, he grabbed my hand.

"I just want to say I really am sorry for the way I acted on the bus."

"It was your pride," I said, not trying to make excuses for his behavior but at least letting him know that I understood it.

"What I didn't tell you is that my situation is a little like your sister Vanessa's."

"How so?"

"My mom left my dad for another family. This rich producer needed a wife to take care of his kids, and my mom signed up, leaving my dad to raise me. She later regretted it and tried to come back. My dad thought about it because I needed a mom, but he said no and has been angry and making bad choices ever since. She's never tried to come back into my life again until now. The whole accident thing brought her out of the woodwork. She says that she's gonna be there for me now, but I just don't know whether I can trust her."

Not quite knowing what to say and not wanting to push him, I stayed quiet. He soon piped up again.

"Why can't my mom be like your mom? You're the center of her world," he said.

"My mom's so embarrassing. Sometimes, when people go to great lengths to show their love, it's unhealthy for them. I need to find her a different job."

"I don't know what all she's doing, but at least her actions show she loves you. She's not just giving you words."

I looked him in the eye and told him what I knew deep down within my soul.

"If you have something to say to your mom, you need to open up and say it respectfully. Don't hold it in. Just be ready for consequences. If you're longing for y'all to be reconciled, don't keep a hard heart because of her past mistakes. We both know time is precious. We're young, and we learned that lesson early in a tragic way, but we learned it nonetheless. I like you, Stone, but I'm not going to walk on eggshells to try to maintain a relationship with you."

"I hear you," he said, shaking his head emphatically up and down to show he understood.

"Good! Then come on and get me some food!"

I wanted to sleep in on Saturday. It had been such a tumultuous week. But my mom wouldn't let me. She was throwing a party for my dad's fortieth birthday, and she enlisted my help. She'd sent him on errands to keep him out of the house while we got everything ready. My parents had always been known for their big shindigs. This year, with my dad having a tough time financially, we hadn't hosted anything. Even though their relationship had been rocky, my mom was going all out.

"Victoria, I just want you to know that I want you to be proud of me. At the same time I really want to help your dad with the finances, so I'm going to be feverishly looking for something else to do. But for now I have quit working for that service."

"That's great, Mom!" I said as I smiled from ear to ear and hugged her tight.

I hated that she was spending money on my dad's party. That was money she could have been saving, but she wanted to show him she loved him in her own special way. She was happy and willing to sacrifice, but she wasn't going to compromise her morals anymore. And I was so relieved.

"Mom, where's all the food for the party?" I said when I went to the kitchen and didn't see where to begin.

"Don't worry, food's coming," my mother replied all bubbly as she pinched my cheeks.

"Mom, you aren't having it catered, are you?" I asked, shuddering at how expensive that would be.

"I got this!"

Vanessa showed up and said what I was

feeling. "This is so nice for you to do for my dad, but he's been a butt. Why are you going all out?"

"You both are teenage girls and have all these guys chasing after you and stuff, and I'm not trying to set a bad example, but remember, I'm married. I have a lot invested in this relationship with your father. He's not perfect. I'm not either, but I'm all in it," she said.

"He's got to do him, deal with things his way. But I got to do me and deal with things my way. If wanting to show him how much I love him means giving him a birthday party, then that's what I am going to do. And that means I need my two favorite girls to make it all nice, and help me play hostess later!"

Because things were tight around the house, the maid service we used to have on a weekly basis hadn't been around in weeks. None of us even realized how dirty the place had become until we all put on our imaginary aprons, as my mother called it, and got busy cleaning. A few hours into being on our knees, scrubbing the floors, bathrooms, and toilets, the doorbell rang. It was too early for anyone to be coming for the party. Maybe it was the caterer that my mom wouldn't admit to. I went to the door to be of assistance. I almost wanted to throw up, not in a bad way, but because I was embarrassed when I saw Stone standing there with his rock star dad!

"Hell-ooo," I drawled, faking calm. If only I could slam the door and start all over by not even answering it. I didn't want them to see me looking a hot mess, with suds in my hair and dust all over me.

"You look fine," Stone said, sensing I was embarrassed.

"Um, yeah?"

"My dad wants to speak to your mom, if that's okay."

"She's okay with everything that happened. You don't have to come and apologize or anything like that," I said, unable to even look at Mr. Bush in my present condition.

"I actually have a proposition for her," the rock star said.

"Okay, she's downstairs in the den, sir."

Stone and his dad went down the hall, and I immediately ran toward my room to try and fix myself up. I bumped right into Vanessa.

"Who's at the door?"

Panicking, I said, "It's Stone and his dad."

"Oh my gosh, you look tore up from the floor up."

"I know!"

"And where are they?"

"They went to see my mom."

"She looks equally messed up. She's going to hate you. You know he's her favorite artist. When I first moved in with you all, she kept singing Sweet Lips' songs and saying how she loved herself some Lars Bush."

I felt bad, but I didn't know what to do. My sister yanked me into her bathroom and started scrubbing my face. She brushed my hair, went into her dirty clothes, pulled out a sweater, sprayed some air freshener on it, and threw it my way. In five minutes, I looked almost good enough to be America's Next Top Model. Vanessa and I couldn't get down to the den fast enough.

When we did, we found my mom deep in conversation with Stone's dad. He looked at me and smiled. My mom looked up at both of us, but she was cool, calm, and collected. Even though she didn't look like she usually did—a stunning princess—she was still beautiful.

We got in the den right as she said, "You want to offer me a job?"

Vanessa nudged me in the arm, and I nudged her back. What in the world was this all about? I looked at Stone, and he winked.

"Yes, we're looking for someone to serve as president of the band's foundation," Mr. Bush answered her.

My mom's eyes widened. "I love charitable organizations. I certainly can plan parties. And I know all the stats on your band, and I can handle PR."

"I want to know if it's something you'd be interested in. I will send a formal offer over on Monday. It's been nice meeting you, and I appreciate your support over the years. I think you'd be a great addition to our team, if you decide to accept the position."

My mom introduced Vanessa to Stone's dad, and Stone came over to me. Truly thankful and shocked, I said, "I was telling you that my mom needed to find a different job, and you put all this together! She loves your dad! This is crazy!"

"He started talking to me about needing someone for this position, and I recommended your mom. He came over to meet her, and they talked it over while you were trying to get all glammed up for some guy."

I hit him in the arm. "My dad's having a birthday party later on. I'd love it if you'd come."

"I'll see what I can work out."

"Oh, nu-uh. If you can come over unannounced, you can certainly show up when I invite you!" We laughed.

Three hours later the guests started arriving. My mom was freaking out because no food had come. Vanessa and I tried repeatedly to get her to tell us who was bringing it, but she kept saying it was a surprise. When my dad's mom pulled up with some of her relatives and brought in chitterlings, fried chicken smothered in gravy, and pigs' feet, my mom smiled from ear to ear, knowing my dad would be in heaven.

My grandma put on an apron and said to my mom, "For you to ask me to come up and do this for my son means so much. I know you thought I hated you. I was just jealous you took my son away, but we got to get past all that. I got a present for him."

My grandma moved out of the way. Vanessa was standing next to me, and our mouths dropped when we saw our brother that we had met down there. He gave us a small wave.

Our grandma uttered, "I know his people, and I been talking to him. Talked some sense into him and told him he needed to come up here and meet his dad properly."

"Grandma, Dad's going to be so excited," Vanessa said as she gave my grandma a big hug.

My grandmother was a busy bee. I wanted to help, but I didn't want to get in the way. Then she caught me looking at her.

"Come on, baby! Show me your room," she said to me, taking my arm. As we walked to my bedroom, she said, "Grandma needs to apologize to you."

"Grandma, you don't have to say a thing. I love you, and I need to get to know you better. I'm so glad you're here. I can't wait to eat your food. It smells so good."

"I know. You couldn't wait to eat when you were at my house the last time, looking at that food like it was gonna put too many pounds on your skinny body. Well, that's what food's supposed to do. Can't be too skinny—got to have some curves. I know you're half white, but hips ain't never hurt nobody."

"Grandma!"

"Don't be shocked. How do you think I got your daddy?" my mom teased, coming in with a camera to take a picture of my grandma and me in my room.

"Victoria, I love you and look forward to getting to know you more," my grandma said.

We laughed and hugged. Then we heard warnings from my sister and relatives downstairs that my dad was coming. We hurried back down to catch the moment, because of course my grandma didn't want to miss seeing her baby.

My dad was so stunned. He hugged his mom. He cried when he saw his son. He blew kisses to Vanessa, Junior, and me, and he took my mom in his arms and spun her around. At that moment I knew they were going to get it all together.

Then a voice I loved hearing said, "Where have you been?"

"Stone, I didn't know you came."

"Yeah, I blended in with the crowd."

"I'm just glad to see you."

"Well, I'm just glad to be here. I know we've only been talking for a week. It sounds pretty crazy to ask this of you, but um, I wanted to know if you'd be my girl?"

"Are you ready for me? It's like I told you: I'm not trying to compromise."

"Victoria House, I like you just the way you are—confident, pretty, and sassy."

I could tell he wanted to kiss me, but I had too many relatives all over the place. So instead he hugged me real tight.

Knowing that I was okay with my mom, my dad, my sister, my guy, and myself, I wanted to hug myself. In just over a week, I realized I controlled my joy. No longer would I be half into anything related to my life. Only being all in would yield the results I wanted. If I didn't like something, I needed to work on it and not allow issues or people to change me for the worse. Finally, I was in a healthy and happy place.

STEPHANIE PERRY MOORE is the author of many YA inspirational fiction titles, including the *Lockwood Lions* series, the *Payton Skky* series, the *Laurel Shadrach* series, the *Perry Skky Jr.* series, the *Yasmin Peace* series, the *Faith Thomas Novelzine* series, the *Carmen Browne* series, the *Morgan Love* series, and the *Beta Gamma Pi* series. Mrs. Moore speaks with young people across the country, encouraging them to achieve every attainable dream. She currently lives in the greater Atlanta area with her husband, Derrick, and their three children. Visit her website at www. stephanieperrymoore.com.

WANT A DIFFERENT
point of view?

JUST *flip* THE BOOK!

Grovehill
GIANTS

The savvy cheer squad at Grovehill High is trying to win state. Their routines are tight, but the girls need to bring it if they are going to win. Coach says one team, one goal, no drama. The fresh guys playing Giants football are tough athletes. But too many prima donnas could keep these awesome ballers from being dynamic and taking it to the Dome.

FRE**S**TONE**H**
Guy

Stone Bush has vowed never to be like his rock star dad. Too busy. Too drunk. Too high. *But now he needs an edge to stay in the game.*

STAND FIRM

Stephanie Perry Moore
& Derrick Moore

SADDLEBACK PUBLISHING

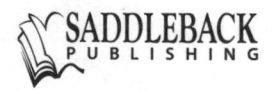

FRESH GUY

Truly Fine

Deep Soul

Quiet Strength

Stand Firm

Man Up

www.sdlback.com

Copyright © 2014 by Saddleback Educational Publishing

ISBN-13: 978-1-62250-686-6
ISBN-10: 1-62250-686-3
eBook: 978-1-61247-751-0

Printed in Guangzhou, China
NOR/1113/CA21302124

18 17 16 15 14   1 2 3 4 5

To Tevin Washington & Vad Lee

Being the quarterback of a D1 school is not an easy job. It's particularly tough when you have to share the responsibility. Thank you for being big enough to understand that doing what was best for your school meant that you both had to rotate in and out of the starting lineup. You both have stood firm and guided your teammates to victory again and again. Know that the school is better because of your leadership.

We are truly proud of you both. We hope every reader strives to be the best they can be as well.

You are great gentlemen. We know more greatness is yet to come!

ACKNOWLEDGEMENTS

When you want an edge, it is natural to be tempted to get that advantage by any means necessary. You don't want to wait months for results. You don't want others to beat you out. You tell yourself you can't afford to be out of the game. However, you cannot truly be a winner if you cheat to make it happen. Have integrity and do not be afraid to work for what you want.

You may be going through a lot because your home life is unstable. Maybe you're the parent in your home. It could be that you feel you have no adult guidance. Or maybe you feel adults have let you down. If so, know you are better than what seems to be holding you back. Learn from the mistakes of the adults around you and do better. Find the way and show someone else how to be better as well. Meaning, we hope you learn from this story that you must stand firm in your beliefs. If you're doing something wrong, stop it. If you want to do what's right, do it. If you know you are worth it, believe it. You are better because of your trials. Learn life's lessons. And live to never repeat past mistakes.

Acknowledgements

Here's a big thank you to those who help us stand firm.

To our parents: Dr. Franklin and Shirley Perry Sr. and Ann Redding, because you really raised us well, we can help our kids stand firm.

To our publisher, especially our designer, Ashley Thompson, because you made sure the covers were real and captured the eye, we know they will stand firm on shelves and make an impact.

To our extended family: brothers, Dennis Perry and Victor Moore, sister, Sherry Moore, godparents, Walter and Marjorie Kimbrough, Jim and Deen Sanders, young nephews, Franklin Perry III, Kadarius Moore, and godsons, Danton Lynn, Dakari Jones, and Dorian Lee, because you are in our lives, we are able to stand firm and tell stories that hopefully will help readers do the same.

To our assistants: Candace Johnson, Shaneen Clay, and Alyxandra Pinkston, because you all help us make deadlines, we can stand firm knowing that the book will be on point.

To our friends who mean so much: Paul and Susan Johnson, Chan and Laurie Gailey, Antonio and Gloria London, Chett and Lakeba Williams, Jay and Deborah Spencer, Bobby and Sarah Lundy, Harry and Torian Colon, Byron and Kim Forest, Donald and Deborah Bradley, Charles

and Kristy Kelly, and Patrick and Krista Nix, because of your friendship, we can stand firm and help others.

To our teens: Dustyn, Sydni, and Sheldyn, because you are ours, we daily stand firm and try to help you become dynamic.

To the media specialists, school administrators, teachers, and educational companies across the country that support us, especially the great folks in Georgia Public Schools, because you support our work, we are able to stand firm and help make our great state academically better for our young people.

To our new readers, who we have faith will reach their goals, because you want to stand firm and get your education, you will.

And to our King, who blesses us daily, because you made us who we are, we can stand firm knowing we are right where you want us and doing just what you want us to do.

Collective Proof

Man, your catch is what caused us to get in scoring position so that I could kick the ball! You're the man," my buddy Emerson Prince, our new kicker, ran up to me and said, before he was surrounded by our teammates.

"But he doesn't know the whole story does he?" an annoying voice said to me. I looked over my shoulder and saw it was Gage, our starting quarterback, all up in my business.

Irritated, I shouted, "Man, what are you talking about?"

Gage had a big smirk on his face. "If it's working for you, who am I to tell? But don't act like you're all that. I know your secret, Stone."

Coach Swords, our head football coach, rushed up to both of us. "I'm real proud of you men, keeping your heads on straight. I've always believed in you all, but I got to admit, when we got the ball on our own three-yard line with less than thirty seconds to play, I thought it was over. But, Gage, you held your composure and didn't panic. You saw an opening and threw to Stone. Your pass was high, but you gave him a chance," he said.

"And, Stone, I have no idea how you caught that ball. You had to jump up about five feet in the air. The last time I gave you the vertical jump test you couldn't even clear two feet. And that was when, July? It was for sure before the season started. Look at you now. This is November. I'm impressed. Some scouts are here tonight from Miami and Alabama. I know they took notice of that move. Great job!"

I could see in Gage's eyes that he didn't like me getting all the accolades. He wasn't even the best quarterback on our team, but because of politics—his dad was the former booster club president, and he obviously had something over our head coach—Gage was allowed to keep his

position in the first place. Gage's pass wasn't just high, it was more than an arm's length away from me, and it favored my opponent's position. He really shouldn't be the starter, and all the ballers knew it.

Our team was mostly composed of black guys, and they felt the coach picked Gage to be quarterback based on race. There was an African American guy named Chaz who was better. He had a longer arm and was quicker on his feet, with blazing speed to get away from defenders. But he was sidelined. The sad part about that was Chaz was a senior and the scouts were here. He wasn't getting the opportunity to shine, and that wasn't cool. Actually many of us white guys on the team felt Gage shouldn't be playing over Chaz as well.

I looked over in the stands at the usual spot where college scouts sat. Instantly, I saw the recruiters Coach Swords had mentioned. It was easy to spot them as they were wearing their school sweatshirts.

Just the thought of potentially going to Alabama or Miami brought a smile to my face—until Gage immediately wiped it off with his sarcasm.

"Like any of those teams would want somebody with your issues."

"Man, don't hate. If you got something to say to me, Gage, if you think you know something, then you need to just say it. I'm not going to stand here and take your unfounded insults."

"Ya see, now you're paranoid and you're telling on yourself. I haven't insulted you at all. The reason my pass to you wasn't pretty was because I was trying to throw the ball away when I threw it way over your head. Your leap was impressive, doggone unnatural. You can't fool someone who's been where you are, Stone," Gage declared.

"It's hard for us to keep up with these black guys. Their natural ability is freaking spooky. That sophomore tight end who runs circles around you in practice is waiting to take your spot. You begged Coach for another opportunity, and I know you did something to make sure you wouldn't blow it."

Completely offended, I frowned and protested, "You have no proof."

Gage leaned in to me and scoffed, "The fact that you're entertaining my suspicions this long is proof enough. You better watch it. Them 'roids are for real."

I pushed Gage, and he fell into some cheer-leaders. He wasn't trying to attack me, fight me back, or make a big deal out of it. He made his point, and I'd already been wounded enough by his words. I wanted to sink to the turf, bury my head in it, and scream out as loud as I could. I hated that Gage was right. I *had* popped a couple of steroid pills. It all started a few weeks back.

My dad, Lars Bush, was the leading vocalist in the hot rock band Sweet Lips. My dad and his band were gearing up to go on a new fall tour. I lived in a mansion on fifty acres. All through grade school I'd gone to private Catholic schools, but when the parents and teachers found out who my dad was, some of them thought I was a heathen, a product of sex, drugs, and rock and roll. My dad didn't like them judging me.

When I was younger and on the little league team, I'd met some of the guys who would be going to Grovehill. So I asked my dad if I could go there for high school. Football-wise, it was stellar, so my dad didn't mind me giving it a try. He was so busy with his own world that he never bothered to ask how the change was working out.

It was just the two of us living in our home. Well, us and Dad's head bodyguard, Thorne. Thorne was like a big brother to me, and in the last year I'd seen him go from two hundred pounds to two fifty. And the added weight was all muscle mass—his upper body was now completely ripped. He told me if there was ever anything he could do for me, to just let him know. I put two and two together: he'd been using chemical help to upgrade his physique. I didn't know how I felt about that at first.

Then I went to football practice, and the sophomore Gage was talking about, Jaboe, completely showed me up. He was catching passes out of the back field that I just couldn't pull off.

Within a few days, Coach brought me in his office, and I'll never forget what he said.

"I'm gonna have to bench you, Stone."

Upset, I cried, "What do you mean, you're going to bench me?"

"Calm down, son. These last games we have are crucial. I've got to play the best players. You've been dropping a lot of passes. You haven't been blocking as hard. It's like you're timid. I need a tight end that's a dual threat. It's not

that you've gotten worse. Jaboe's just gotten better. I haven't seen any improvements, Stone, so I'm going to make the switch."

What was I supposed to say to that? How was I supposed to respond? It wasn't in me to whine like a baby, but I had to plead with Coach to give me another try. When I left his office that dreadful day I was determined to prove to him that I could do it. But how *could* I do it without assistance? I went to the only man I knew who could help me—Thorne. If he'd beefed up his physique in a short amount of time to better handle cronies and goons, then he had to help me.

"You sure you want to do this?" he sort of laughed at me and said. "Because I don't know, man. If your dad found out—"

"He's not gonna find out. I *can't* lose my starting job. My dad's got me at this school for football. He's a star on stage. I gotta be a star on the field to keep his attention, you know what I'm saying."

"I hear you, but I just don't want you to get hooked on something you can't get off of."

"I just need a little boost to make me explode a little harder, jump a little higher, do my thing so Coach will get off my back. That's all."

Giving in, Thorne said, "Okay I'm just going to give you a few pills. That's it. I'm not trying to start a drug habit in a kid. I could lose my job."

"I got you."

"But I need to warn you. There might be some side effects."

Squinting, I inquired, "What do you mean? They're going to make me bigger, faster, and stronger, right?"

"Yeah, the pills should do that, but you might have some night sweats. You might not be able to sleep. You might gain weight in places you don't want to. I'm just saying. When you take shortcuts, there are risks. You willing to pay the price?"

Not caring about the risks, I said, "Yes."

I snatched the pills out of his hands, and for the last two weeks I'd been dominant. But now that Gage was calling me out and I was getting accolades unjustly, the old me with the conscience was having issues. Scouts liked what they saw, but if I was found out, I'd lose more than my starting job. I had to figure this out.

There's nothing like seeing a pretty girl to get your mind off your troubles. The gorgeous Victoria

House was standing about ten feet away from me. Acting on impulse, I picked her up and spun her around in celebration. But she got all offended, so I put her down. When I looked over at her again, I didn't know if her cheerleading skirt was actually falling down or if it appeared to be coming off since that was my inward desire. Either way, her legs looked so dang firm and lovely.

Her lips had me going too. She was talking to her half sister, Vanessa, who was dating my boy Emerson. Vanessa was ecstatic that he'd just won the game for us with his monster kick. Nah, actually I think it was Victoria's smile that got me. It was so coy, yet so innocent. For a moment I thought she was smiling back at me, but as soon as our eyes locked, she abruptly turned the other way. I couldn't figure it out. Why was this girl getting to me? I was jolted out of my wonderings when I felt someone sock me in the shoulder. I quickly turned and was about to take the culprit down until I saw it was Emerson.

"I know you won the game and all, but shoot, man, that hurt."

"Dang, man, why you so sensitive?" Emerson said.

I really couldn't explain it. Maybe the steroids were having an impact. Thorne had told me to watch out for side effects, but because I was excited about seeing the positive results I wanted from the drugs, I didn't mind having the dry mouth, the difficulty sleeping, and the increased irritability. I now knew what it was like being a girl on her cycle, having mood swings. My body was sensitive to the touch. But while those were things I was going to have to watch out for and try to keep under control, I wasn't ready to give up this major feeling of being stronger than I'd ever been.

"Settle down, dude," Emerson said, noticing how antsy I was. "You hungry?"

"Nah."

"Not hungry? As big as you're getting? If you ain't eating, how you getting buff like that? With those bulging muscles you should be hungry all the time. What you trying to be? The Incredible Hulk or something?"

Emerson and I were around each other all the time, but he wasn't a big talker. Now that he had won the game and we found out he was the kicker making field goals from the fifty-yard

line, it gave him swagger. But he was thinking what he was supposed to about me: that I was getting big because I'd been eating more and drinking protein shakes and stuff.

And I had to keep up the facade, so I quickly picked up his line and said, "Yeah, yeah. What we going to eat? Pasta, pizza, what? I need something that's going to stick to these ribs."

"Yeah, pizza sounds good. Some of the others are going to get some at Chuck E. Cheese's."

I teased, "I figured that much. Now that you got a girlfriend, you ain't going to let her go nowhere without you."

"Ha-ha-ha," Emerson said, unable to hide the fact that he was sprung. "You better quit being a player. I see you looking at my girl's sister. Y'all make goo-goo eyes at each other every time we have lit class."

"I don't know what you're talking about."

"Quit denying it, man. Just go on over there and talk to the girl. You want me to loan you my ..."

He moved his hand over the cup in his britches. Laughing, I said, "Watch it now. You on your first girl. Don't be getting all cocky. Don't let success make you crazy."

I didn't need any help when it came to the ladies, though I wasn't a player like my boy Ryder Packer. He was the starting linebacker, and he got mad respect from the players and the girls. But I wasn't like Emerson either, just on my first girlfriend. I didn't know if I wanted to be tied down.

However, there was something about Victoria that I just couldn't shake. Maybe it was her golden skin. I'd never dated outside my race, and though Victoria wasn't all black, she wasn't completely white either. She was biracial. Her mom was white and the dad she shared with Vanessa was African American.

I didn't think color mattered, but I'd never been as attracted to any girl as I was to Victoria. So maybe straight-up Caucasian girls weren't my type, or maybe Victoria could have been hot pink and she still would have pulled me in hard with her savvy flair. The girl had my number. She had me figured out for real. Whatever it was, I was planning to let her know we needed to get to the bottom of what was going on between us.

Unfortunately, high-maintenance cheer-leader Jillian Grayson chose that moment to get

in the way. She sidled up to me, smiling at me like I was her man, and blocked me from talking to Victoria. She was a stuck up dumb blonde who wasn't even naturally blonde.

My heart was starting to beat so hard. Maybe all the excitement had gotten to me, or I might have just been hungry. I was hearing what the two of them were saying, but I couldn't really make any sense out of it until I saw Victoria dash away, like Jillian had said or done something to hurt her feelings. Not wanting any part of the girl drama, I left to get some water. I caught the water boy just in time. I felt like I was having a heart attack. I sat down on the bench and hit the tub.

"Stone, you all right? Do I need to get the coach, the trainer, or the paramedics?" Jillian asked.

But after I gulped down the water and took a few deep breaths, I started feeling better.

"No, I'm straight. I'm straight."

"I can help you get to your car," she said in an alluring way.

I wanted her to stay far away from me. I was trying to make my move with Victoria, but

when I stood up, I wobbled back down a little, and my arm somehow ended up around Jillian's shoulder.

"I'm okay," I said, though I really wasn't.

"Oh, you're more than okay. You're fine," Jillian said as she gave my butt a possessive squeeze.

"Jill, come on, girl."

"What? I like you."

Jillian was a very high maintenance girl. Not only did we all know she was a brat, but she was also still going out with my buddy ER. He used to be the kicker on the team before he moved away. He didn't move to another state or anything, just twenty miles away near down-town Atlanta. So he and Jillian hadn't broken up. But they were polar opposites. He was real nice, sweet, and easy-going. She was truly mean and nasty.

"Look, Jill, you got to keep your hands to yourself."

"Why?" she said, trying to be all seductive.

" 'Cause you don't want to start nothing you can't finish," I said, attempting to remind her that she already had a boyfriend.

I dashed into the locker room so that I could change. I was getting some dirty looks from the other players, but I tried to ignore them. I thought that maybe I was being paranoid.

Fifteen minutes later I headed out to the parking lot. When I reached my car, I found Jillian leaning up against it.

"Can I get in?" I said when she wouldn't move.

"You can move me."

"Come on now. I got to go, Jillian."

"You're going with everybody to eat, right?"

"Yeah, and they've already left."

"Right, that's why I need to ride with you," Jillian whined.

"You're going?" I said, fervently hoping that was not the case.

"Uh, duh. Yeah."

She took the key out of my hand and unlocked the door, letting her behind, or lack thereof, rub up against my zipper. Quickly, I moved back. I didn't want any part of what this girl was putting down.

"I'll give you a ride but—"

"But what?" she said as she opened the driver's door and crawled over to the passenger's side.

"Let's keep our distance."

I was just trying to get her there with as little interaction as possible. I wasn't paying her any attention as I drove. The last thing I wanted to do was give her any reason to think I liked her.

"Let's not get there too soon," she said about five miles into the drive.

I looked over, and she was shirtless. "What are you doing?!" I cried.

"What? I know you like what you see." She was licking her lips like she wanted to eat me up. "I'm ready to finish what we started."

I pulled into the nearest place I could find—some convenience store parking lot—and said, "Look, I don't know what made you think I was into you, but I thought I was clear. You're dating ER."

"He doesn't own me."

"Well, I'm not trying to get with you," I said, throwing up my hands in exasperation. Taking my one hand, I rooted around the back of the car, found her shirt, and handed it to her. She snatched it from me. I could tell she was mad, but you know where she was mad? In her

own seat. She put the top back on. I was fine. She got it.

"You got to be kidding me! All I want to do is go to sleep, and my dad's having a party? Seriously?" I vented as I pulled into our estate Saturday night. I was coming from the cheer competition, where I'd felt out of my element.

The day had been draining. At first I thought it'd be fun to see girls flip upside down so us guys could sneak a few peeks. But I wasn't as into that as I thought I'd be. I wanted to talk to Victoria, but she seemed pretty ticked with me. Then she nearly fainted, and Emerson had driven her, her mom, and her little brother, Junior, home early. I'd gone over to help her get in the car, but then I was stuck hanging out at the gym since Coach wanted us to support the squad.

After the meet, we had mandatory practice. Since we would be missing a practice the upcoming week because of a teachers' workday, he was getting it in early. I was exhausted, and now I had to deal with this drama at home.

Cars were parked from the entrance gate all the way around our circular drive. Before I even

walked inside, I could hear the noise practically swaying our house from side to side. I knew right away I wasn't gonna get any sleep that night.

As soon as I got in the door, I was accosted by Bishop, my dad's guitar player.

"What's up, squirt?" Bishop said, catching me in a headlock and rubbing his knuckles real hard on the top of my head. He'd always hated me.

Instinctively, I pushed him in the gut. He slammed into a wall, and when the guests surrounding him started giving me props, he wanted to make me look stupid.

"Someone thinks he's the man. You oughta bring some girls around to back it up," he taunted me.

"I need no advice from the man who's always burning," I retorted, shutting him down.

Giggles erupted from the cute women parading around in bathing suits and short-shorts. They left Bishop's side and walked my way. He got real angry. His stoned eyes turned blood red. I just looked at him with pity. He was the one who'd taught me how to snap at people. Growing up, I got tired of being the butt of his jokes. Thorne sat me down and told me Bishop was

jealous of me because my dad was the star of the band. He really couldn't hate on my dad or he'd get kicked out. He thought he should be second in line for the world's attention, but I became the star since my dad was a single father. Not that I wanted the spotlight, but it didn't shine Bishop's way. He resented me ever since.

"Hey, Heather, how you doing?" I said as I spotted my dad's girlfriend looking out the living room windows.

Out back was a big open barnyard ballroom. Most of the people weren't in our house. Heather seemed even more irritated than I was about the party. In addition to being his girlfriend, she also managed my dad's foundation. I really felt sorry for her. My dad dogged her out so bad. I guess my mom running out on us had hurt him so much that he could never fully commit to anyone. Heather thought he was her boyfriend, but he was so unfaithful, and she knew it. Why'd she put up with it?

"You're not out there partying?"

"No. I thought we were going to have a special celebration alone. But your dad's changing. I don't even know how much he wants me around anymore."

"What do you mean?" I said, knowing that Heather was one of the best things in his life.

When she wasn't around, he was too wild. I'd walked in on him a number of times and found him just as stoned as Bishop. He promised me this tour would be different, but with Heather not around, I knew that it wasn't going to be easy for him to stay an upstanding, law-abiding citizen. He claimed that drugs made him crazy, and he needed that edge to stay hot for his fans. But I wanted a father, and if he was locked up— or worse, dead—how could that help me?

"You know, I'm just worried about your dad," Heather said.

"Well, what do you mean?" I asked again, raising my voice over the loud music that seemed to get louder by the second.

" 'Cause, he's taking uppers to stay up, and then he takes downers to go down. I probably shouldn't be telling his son this, but he doesn't even know where some of the drugs are coming from. And since he won't listen to me, I don't want to be around."

I was so mad you would have thought I'd gone out to the driveway and found my tires

slashed. My dad and I had talked about him living on the edge, and I had to make him honor his commitment to me. If nobody around him was going to make him stop doing dumb, irrational, foolish things, then I had to step up and be the parent. I don't know if it was the steroids or if I'd just had about all I could take of my dad's behavior; whatever the case, I was upset. I started walking hard, stomping through the house, with Heather following after me.

"No, no, no, you can't go in there. You can't tell him I said anything."

"Heather, you and I both know my dad's got heart problems. He already lives on the edge as an artist. I'm not going to sit by and say nothing."

I rushed into the crowded room to clear it out, but I found the people inside in a state of panic. It was pandemonium, and I didn't understand why until I got through the crowd and saw my dad lying on the floor as if he were sleeping. But he wasn't getting any Zs.

"Thorne!" I screamed out, wanting to find my dad's closest friend and bodyguard. When I couldn't find him, I shouted, "Somebody find

Thorne. Can't y'all see something's wrong with my dad?"

Other security guys were trying to push back the people who were crowding in on my father. Everyone there wanted to see. However, he needed room to breathe. I needed to see him breathe—but he wasn't.

"What's going on with him? What happened? Talk to me! Tell me something! Somebody give me a phone! We got to call the paramedics!" I said, before realizing my phone was in my back pocket.

I started to pull my phone out, then immediately dropped it when I saw drug paraphernalia. Yeah, my dad was mixing all kinds of things. I'd told him he had to stop before it was too late, but he didn't listen, and now it might have cost him everything. I was scared out of my mind for my father and for myself. Any drugs that aren't prescribed by a doctor are bad for you. And if any of the folks helplessly looking on didn't understand that, including myself, my dad's unresponsive body lying before us was the collective proof.

Serious Setback

My head was pounding. My heart was racing, and my glands were sweating something fierce as I sat there and watched my dad lying cold in front of me. This couldn't be the end. He had to pull through. Though our relationship was tumultuous, he was my everything. Famous Lars Bush, lead singer of Sweet Lips to the world, but doctor, provider, caregiver, and everything in between to me. Though my mom was still alive, for practical purposes she was gone from my life. I just couldn't lose my dad.

I was an athlete. I thought I was tough, but right then, I was unsure of what to do. Thinking

that it was over, that my world as I knew it would be altered forever, I cried like a baby.

"Get back! Get back! Get back!" Thorne yelled out as he took a big pitcher of water and dumped it on my father.

Instantly and fortunately, he came to. I didn't know what he took, but Thorne knew the water would work. My dad shook his head, flapping his hair like a wet dog trying to dry off.

"Wow, man! What a ride!" he said, making absolutely no sense.

He'd enjoyed his trip, while I'd been in complete anguish.

"Okay, everybody, the party's over. Lars's gonna be fine. You won't be able to leave until we see your cell phones. None of what you saw here tonight can leak. You all signed confidentiality agreements before you came in. We will sue you for any breach."

"Hey, Stone. When did you get home, son?" my dad said in a giggly manner, trying to get himself together as the room cleared out.

Someone must have told Heather what happened because she rushed to his side. As she went to help him up, he pulled her on top of his

lap and started kissing her like he was trying to get down to business right there.

"Lars, stop," Heather said. My dad wouldn't let her go. "Stop it!" Then she slapped him.

Abruptly, he pushed her off of him. My father used to joke that he named me Stone because when I was conceived, that's what he and my mom were—high as a kite. But it was time for all this to stop. He didn't realize how his actions were hurting himself and others. Heather started to cry, and I helped her to her feet. When my dad had the audacity to laugh, I rushed over to him and put my hands around his throat.

"How can you push a lady? How can you insult her like that? She's your girlfriend, Dad. You're so out of your mind you don't even realize what you're messing up."

The fact that my father was still weak didn't occur to me. I wasn't trying to kill him, just choke some sense into him.

Heather took my hand. "No, please no. It's okay. I told you I was leaving anyway, Stone, and that's just what I'm gonna do. I can't take this anymore."

My dad quickly rose to his feet, and though he was stumbling, he made his way over to her, trying desperately to apologize.

"Get off me, Lars. I care about you. I put my heart into you and our relationship, and this is how you treat me."

My dad said, "No, no, I love you, baby. It was just a little party for the tour. That's all."

"But you said you were going to stop," Heather desperately uttered.

"Yeah, Dad. You said you were going to stop," I angrily reminded him.

My dad motioned for me to chill. He then looked at Heather and started pleading. "Don't leave me, baby. I need you for this tour. You know I do. I'll be up in just a second. Please, let's talk about this." He motioned for one of the security guards to help. That little sly signal meant, "Take her to my bedroom." Then he turned back to the rest of us. "Somebody, come on, please tighten this thing up on my arm."

Heather appeared to want to start crying again. Shucks, watching my dad think only of his habit made me want to shed tears of sorrow as well. He was a star, but he was acting

like a junkie. I couldn't believe his arm was outstretched. He seriously wanted help getting high. Hadn't the scare he had just survived put some common sense into him? Obviously not, because he was still acting stupid.

Bishop, who probably would have liked nothing better than for my dad to be out of the picture so he could take over and be the star of the band, stepped up to my father. He tightened the rubber knot around my dad's arm. He was looking right at me as he did this, and I could tell he took pleasure in the fact that watching this was stressful and unnerving for me.

"Yeah, you've always got to have a little something to take the edge off of what's got you down," Bishop mouthed off. "I taught you well."

"I don't want too much of the stuff you just gave me."

"No, no, no, I know. It probably wasn't mixed right."

I didn't know what they were talking about, but I couldn't watch my dad get high again.

"Get out!" I howled at Bishop.

Appalled at my antics, my dad yelled, "Son, what are you doing?"

By this point it was just a few security guards and the other members of my dad's band left in the room. I didn't know if he needed to be the big man in front of them or if he was truly upset. Either way he let me have it something fierce.

"Son, I'm tired of you thinking you can come into my sets and talk to me like I'm the child and you're the parent. God da—" He started using all types of profanity.

As he continued cussing me out, something inside of me grew like a baby chicken does in an egg. When I could take no more, I hatched my fury on him. I balled my hand into a fist and aimed it at his mouth. Before I could actually make contact with my dad, Thorne's palm clasped my fist.

Thorne took my arm, put it behind my back, and held it there. I yanked it real hard, to no avail.

"Have you lost your mind, man? Like I'm going to stand here and let you do that. You need to settle down, Stone. I don't want to have to handle you."

"Let me go, Thorne! Let me go!"

"Yeah, let him go!" Bishop jeered. "He only thinks he's a man. Little weak boy, we can't do nothing with you. Lars, what's up?" Bishop

smiled in a crafty way at me, like, *You haven't stopped anything, and your dad is too stupid to stop himself.* But the last laugh was on Bishop when my dad spoke.

My father said, "I'm cool. My son spoiled it. I'm going to go upstairs and get my other fix on, you know?"

"Let me go, Thorne!" I said, trying to wrestle my way out of his firm grip.

I was so angry. I kept struggling, but I still could not free myself. This had to stop.

"I'm going to let you go, but you need to calm down. I'm serious now. I got your dad."

"Oh, you have him, do you? He's practically dead, and you were just going to stand there and let him use again."

Thorne looked at me like I had a good point. He loosened his grip, and I finally wrenched myself away. I went to my room and paced back and forth. I was so angry, and I felt so weak. I didn't want to use steroids anymore, and I didn't want any help. I felt guilty, but I wanted to be able to deal with it myself.

To fight my dad, I first had to fight Thorne. However, I was too weak. I was a little taller

than Thorne and a little heavier, but he had something else on the inside—a little something that I wanted. So despite what I knew was right, I took two pills that night, instead of the one pill I'd been taking. I didn't even bother to go to the kitchen and get water. Instead I went to the bathroom, put my head underneath the sink, filled my mouth up, and swallowed the pills down. But when I straightened up I had to face myself in the mirror. I'd taken a step back, but so be it.

Hours later, I was unable to sleep. I was tossing and turning in my bed. I was sweating profusely, and I felt like punching a hole in the wall. None of this had anything to do with my dad. I knew it was because I had taken an extra dose of something I should have left alone in the first place.

Shucks, I felt backed into a corner, like I had no other options. I didn't like being called a punk, and I especially didn't like feeling like one. I was getting overheated. My throat was dry, and it felt like my veins were about to pop out. The transformation my body was going through reminded me of the Incredible Hulk.

No, my muscles weren't bulging out that big, but I felt like I was turning into a monster. Then there was a knock on my door.

"Yeah?" I said, already overly agitated.

"Son, I want to come in." It was my father speaking in a real caring tone.

"The door is unlocked, Dad."

He came in, shutting the door softly behind him. His head was hung low, and I could tell he was remorseful about what had gone down earlier.

"Look, man, I just wanted to come see how you're doing."

"How I'm doing? The question is how are *you* doing?"

"Well, I heard you huffing and puffing and wailing, all kinds of crazy noises. You all right?"

"Maybe I drifted off to sleep and didn't realize it."

I wasn't all right, but the last person I could talk to about what I was going through was my father, who was far worse than me when it came to abusing drugs.

"Look, son, I know I scared you tonight. That wasn't my intent. I just need you to relax.

If you want me to start treating you more like an adult, then maybe I need to help you chill. I got a little surprise for you."

It was completely dark outside, but the moonlight through my window illuminated his wide grin.

Pleasantly shocked, I said, "A surprise? What? You didn't have to do anything, Dad. I just want you to stop doing the drugs, the partying. I mean, you're not seventeen. That's me."

"In what book does it say you can't party at my age? That's what I'm saying, son. You're young, but you don't live like it. I've got the perfect gift to help with that."

He was my father, but he had no idea what I did. He didn't come to my football games. I couldn't remember the last time he'd asked me for a report card. Though I was doing well at both my sport and school, if I wasn't, he wouldn't have cared.

"Just do me a favor and be open, okay?"

Not knowing what he was up to but happy he was at least more sane, I nodded.

"That's my boy." Then, like a thief in the night, he quickly disappeared.

I was trying to breathe in deeply, just to slow my heart rate down. I wasn't even tripping over what kind of surprise my father had for me. He loved bringing me the latest gadgets because money was no object, and he tried a bunch of things for himself. Whenever we had a falling out, he would go in his closet and give me something of his. What meant more than anything was the fact that he wanted to make up with me and do something special, and because of that, I smiled just a little.

"Oh, I like that smile," a sexy female voice whispered.

"Yeah, your grin is so nice," another girl said.

I looked over, and one gorgeous body was standing right beside me. I felt the covers move, and I saw the other girl was in my bed, crawling up toward me. I yanked the covers back in place and curled myself away from both of them.

"What are you guys doing here? What is this? I don't understand. Who are y'all, and why are you in my room?"

"Calm down," said the brunette.

"Yeah, relax," the blonde one said.

"You guys got the wrong room. I'm not Lars."

"We know who you are," the Marilyn Monroe look alike said to me. "We're your dad's gift."

"No thanks."

I hoisted myself out of the bed and quickly grabbed my robe from the back of my door.

"Wait. Where are you going? We just want to have a little fun," one of them said.

I was so upset, so tense, so uneasy, and grossed out. Just when I thought my father understood me, that he was sorry for being more of a bad influence than a father, he went and blew it. I didn't care what time of night it was or what he was doing. He needed to know how I felt.

"Leave, you guys. Stop!" I had to go find my dad. I was pissed. "Dad, where are you? Where are you?" I yelled out. I went into his bedroom, but he wasn't there.

I saw a light coming from my dad's office. I stopped in my tracks when I heard him say, "What do you mean, money has gone missing? You need to go back and count it again. There's no way she's stealing."

It was always something with my dad. I didn't know if it was his being a rocker that made drama follow him everywhere or if he just

had plain old bad luck in that regard. Right then I was too upset to care. He was going through what appeared to be a financial crisis. Well, the crisis he had with his son was far bigger. So I stepped in his doorway.

"I'll call you back," he said to whoever was on the other end of the line when he saw me. "How long have you been standing there?"

"Does it matter?" I said with attitude, bucking my shoulders up at him, still pissed.

"Dang, son, you're pretty fast. I sent you two in there. I didn't think you'd be done this fast. What? You came to say thanks?"

"To thank you? Are you kidding me?"

"What are you talking about, Stone? I'm tired. I'm having to deal with one thing after another, and you're coming up in here acting like you're upset at me about something. I gave you a gift."

"Dad, what kind of father gives his teenage son two girls? It's sick."

He stepped back for a moment. He didn't quite know how to respond. He was looking at me like he was trying to figure out if I was serious.

"I'm a good dad. You want for nothing, Stone. You've basically had a silver spoon in your mouth since you were born."

"What you call a blessing, I call a curse. The road has changed you. The fans are giving you a warped perception of yourself, and the drugs ... I don't even need to talk about the drugs."

"All right, son. I thought we dealt with this earlier tonight. You're not the parent."

"I feel like I am, Dad."

"Are you gay?"

"What did you say?" I said. What was this, the Dark Ages? My dad was in a time warp.

My father shot back, "You heard me, Stone. I'm just saying you must be gay. I never see you with any girls, then I send some women your way, and you come crying to me."

"Everything okay in here?" My dad's escalating voice brought Thorne into his office.

"I don't know. What would you do if you found out your boy was fruity?"

I realized that my dad was officially crazy and a homophobe, but he was making me feel like a maniac on the inside.

"What is *wrong* with you?" I screamed.

"What kind of father are you? Why do you think this is rational behavior? What are you doing? I need a father. I don't even know why Mom—"

"What? You don't understand why she left you with me? Because she didn't want you, son. I don't like saying it, but it's the truth."

"Like I didn't know that."

"Well, don't make me feel like what I give you and who I am aren't good enough. I'm the only parent you got—the only one who loves you enough to stick around."

"When you're gone most of the time, how is that sticking around? Do you really think I'm worthless because I have no desire to be some rocker following in your footsteps? You never come to my football games," I said, absolutely upset and angry.

He had the nerve to say, "You never ask me."

I looked at Thorne like, *Can you believe him? Say something!* But he only held my gaze for a moment before looking away. He didn't have my back where my dad was concerned. I'd have to deal with my father myself.

Turning back to him, I said, "Why should I have to ask you? The fathers of the other boys on

the team live, eat, and breathe football. They're there at our practices. They watch film with their sons at night. They're trying to help them get scholarships. They're all in, and it seems like you're involved with everything *but* my life."

My dad's neck glands were bulging as he seethed in anger. He said, "Well, son, those fathers aren't me. They may have no other option but to encourage their kids to get scholarships so they can go to school. I work so that you don't have to do anything in this life that you don't want to. You don't have to be me, but everything you have comes from me. I'm sick and tired of you not respecting that, treating me like being a rocker makes me ignorant. It seems like I can't get anything right with you. I love you, but boy do I—"

"What? Hate me?" I offered, wanting him to just come out with it.

Sighing, he said, "I wasn't trying to say that, son."

"You know what? You don't have to say it."

I abruptly turned and left his office, slamming the door behind me. My dad and I would never be tight, and at that moment, I knew it. We'd just suffered a serious setback.

CHAPTER THREE

Lay Off

I'm serious, Thorne! Get off of me!" I said all groggy the next morning as Thorne annoyingly tried to wake me up.

Little did he know I wasn't asleep anyway. I'd tossed and turned all night, unable to get comfortable. It was no wonder I had fussed with my dad, tussled with Thorne, and just ended up feeling like an idiot. Though I was mentally drained, my body physically wouldn't shut down. My mind would start wondering about how I could get out of this rut, and my body seemed to still be working overtime from what I had ingested. So, there was no rest for the weary.

It was Sunday morning, and I wanted to sleep in. I figured if I just lay there, I would doze off to sleep. But Thorne had other plans. He pulled off the covers and yanked my entire body out of the bed.

"Let's go. We're going to work out," Thorne announced as he plucked me in the head.

Throwing his hand off my head, I said, "No, I'm not doing that."

"Yeah you are," he said.

"You think I want to work out with you? I get it. You're bigger and stronger. Now leave me alone."

"You know I can't do that."

"Why? Did my dad send you in here? Let me guess: he's afraid that I'm too weak, and he's put you on the job of making me tougher."

"This has nothing to do with your dad. You know you and I got our own thing. You're like my little brother."

"I wasn't like your little brother last night. If you think I want to hang out with you like nothing happened, then you got a screw loose that you need to tighten. The place I had for you in my heart? Gone." Our eyes locked, and he saw

my anger. He folded his arms, signaling that he didn't know what to do with me. I was unmoved. "I'm serious, Thorne, man."

"Last night I was doing my job. Today, I want to do my duty."

"I don't understand," I said, completely frustrated.

"I care about you, Stone, and I'm noticing something going on with you that I don't like. We need to talk about it, and we're going to talk about it right now." I had some jogging pants hanging over the end of my bed. He picked them up and tossed them to me. "Let's go."

Seeing that I had no other choice, I grudgingly complied. There were three gyms in our area. One was at my house, and we only used it when a serious workout wasn't needed. The second was LA Fitness. We went there when we wanted to see all the girls. Gold's Gym was where we worked out when we were trying to get down to business and get buff. Just because I felt forced to go didn't mean I had to open up, so I said nothing. But I did have to admit I liked the way Thorne worked out. He pushed himself. He attacked each apparatus and conquered it.

I could tell he was doing more reps than he actually wanted to. He beat his body with his mind.

I was staring at him, and I guess he caught my gaze because he said, "I haven't been on steroids for two years." I didn't know how he knew that's what I'd been wondering about. I also wasn't sure that he was telling the truth, but he insisted, "They were starting to do crazy things to me, Stone. My mind was starting to play tricks on me, and I couldn't even perform down there."

I must have looked shocked because he confirmed it. "That was messed up; but the look I loved, the steroids provided. So I had to make a decision: my physique or my health? I gave up the pills and started coming here every other day. I have since regained and maintained that look through my own hard work."

I still didn't say anything, but I looked at him with newfound respect. He looked me in the eye.

"I owe you an apology for giving you those pills. I don't want you going down the wrong path. It's been eating me up ever since I gave

them to you, and I've watched you change from a caring guy to a beast. That's all right on the football field. I saw you the other night making catches."

"You did?" I asked, totally shocked, but inwardly pleased too.

"Only Superman could have swung in and grabbed you."

"You were at the game?" I questioned, still not believing he was there.

Nodding, Thorne said, "Yes, a couple of weeks ago. I was in the stands cheering you on."

"Did Dad come?"

When Thorne didn't respond right away, I knew the answer was no. "He wanted to, but you know he's been getting ready for this tour. He wanted me to be there."

"That's not true. You wanted to be there."

"It was both."

"All right."

Thorne said, "I'm not here to defend your father. Both of us should be role models in your life, and we both failed you. Your dad's working on him, and I got to work on me. We both owe you more than we're giving, and I just wanted

to spend some time with you to let you know that."

"Well, I don't need your sympathy 'cause if a big brother is gonna treat me how you did last night, I'm fine with being an only child. Besides, with a dad like mine and a mom who's out of the picture, I actually feel like an orphan. He wasn't supposed to be doing drugs anymore, Thorne. He was supposed to be done. He's going to kill himself," I uttered, wishing I didn't care, but knowing deep inside that I did.

"We're gonna get it right. He's gonna get it right. I just wanted to tell you that your dad's got some money problems and relationship problems. This tour has got to do well, or the label might drop him. It's just a lot of pressure. He gets tired and wants to get away from it all. I know it's not right. But what about you and the steroids? Do you want to keep being that good without them? Because if you do, and I know you do, I can help you, train you, and get you right without all that."

"Well, that's what I thought I wanted!" I got up off of the bench and yelled. "Shoot, until last night, that is. You threw your strength in my

face, and it made me want to be big instantly. I went and popped a double dose of the pills."

"You did what?" Thorne looked stunned and disappointed.

"It's not gonna do nothing to me."

"Have you slept, boy? I'm surprised your heart ain't pounding out of your chest."

Being real, I said, "I felt a little weird, but I just don't like to be punked. That's all."

"Taking even more drugs is a punk move."

"It's gonna wear off. It's just a little hard to breathe."

"Exactly. You need to drink a lot of water and leave those pills alone."

"You've been to the game. You've seen it. I've been a difference maker. I can do stuff now that I've never been able to do. I shaved some time off my forty, and my vertical is higher. In the game that edge is gonna help me get five stars."

"What are you talking about?"

"In football, all of the collegiate scouts give rankings to juniors. For your upcoming senior year if you don't have four or five stars, you pretty much can't write your own ticket. Some

three stars have good opportunities, but four and five stars are in demand."

"But when those schools test you—and I'm sure they will—and you got steroids in your system, you'll be black balled, and no school in the country will want you. You won't like that feeling. I'm telling you because that's how I felt this morning, knowing that you probably wouldn't want anything to do with me anymore after last night. Not a cool feeling. So, I'm trying to find you a better way to fix it."

Wow, Thorne really did care. He took me through the wringer; now he wanted to pull me even further to bring me out on a better side. It sounded good in theory, but I wasn't sure that giving up the steroids and the results they brought was something I'd be able to do. But with him caring so much, and with my integrity still deep inside me somewhere yelling out for me to try, maybe there was hope.

"So what? You're going to stay mad at me forever?" Thorne said as we ate breakfast at Cracker Barrel.

"Aw, come on, Stone, you've gotta forgive me. You know I care about you and your dad. In order to really help your dad and take some of his stress away, you and I need to be allies and attack this thing together."

Now Thorne was speaking my language. I didn't need his little apologies; I could have driven my own self to get breakfast. But his help with my father was not something I could pass up.

"How are we going to talk to him? What are we going to say?"

"We'll get to your dad and talk about all that, but right now I want to talk about you. You seem pretty offended by everything your dad did, like sending those girls to your room. Do you have a girl or something?"

I wanted to tell Thorne about Victoria House—the girl who had my interest—but there was nothing going on between us. I just kept thinking about her. My hesitation must have told him there was something going on, though.

"Oh, come on. Talk to me. Tell me."

"No, it's just a girl I like."

"Well, go for it."

"I don't know if I'm her type."

"If you don't make a move, you're never going to know. One thing I learned about you from last night is you definitely got balls. So talk to her, ask her out, man up. Do something."

I cracked a smile. Thorne and I enjoyed our breakfast. We came to the understanding that we were going to talk to my dad about his issues.

When we pulled up to the house, I said to Thorne, "So we're going to talk to him together, and you're not going to back down. We got this, right?"

"Yeah, yeah, we're going to talk to your dad. For sure."

As soon as Thorne and I entered my house, we had every intention of calling a meeting with my dad. We wanted to do an intervention, so to speak, but we couldn't have a heated discussion with him because he was already in one with Heather. She picked up the lamp sitting on the end table and was about to throw it at my dad, but Thorne came in just in time to grab it. I stepped in front of Heather so that she wouldn't be harmed. Heck, I didn't know if she would be harmed by my dad or Thorne, but I knew between

the two of them I needed to protect her because she wasn't safe, not acting like that anyway.

"You better step in front of her, son," my dad went off and said as he got close to my face. "Really, Heather, stealing from me? You think it's okay that one hundred eighty grand is gone?"

"I had to take it! I had to steal it!"

"At least you're admitting it now."

I turned away from her after hearing that, and I think Heather knew how disappointed I was. She and I had been bonding. She had been taking on the role of my mom. The very possibility that she would steal from my father hurt in ways that I couldn't explain, and a part of me wanted to step out of the way and let her fend for herself. Stealing? Really?

"Stone, don't look at me like that. I can explain."

"How?"

I stood there waiting for her to say something, though I felt there was no explanation. However, if she was willing to give me one, I would hear her out; the last thing I wanted was to hate her. But the way it was looking, I wasn't sure that could be avoided.

"Put yourself in my shoes, Stone," Heather pleaded.

"I can't believe you're getting my son involved in all this," my dad shouted.

Heather cried, "We were breaking up. I couldn't take it."

My father looked at her like she was pathetic. "That doesn't justify a theft."

"Please let me explain!" she said, looking at me beseechingly.

"Go ahead," I said, not even paying any attention to my dad because, at that moment, I didn't want my own personal dream to be shattered. "Please explain."

Heather reluctantly continued, "We were supposed to be building a life, your father and me. I wanted to raise you, be a mom, you know? It's been a few years now, and he's never really committed to me. He just cheated on me and humiliated me."

"How dare you tell my son our business!" my dad said, outraged. I could tell he was for sure done with her at that point.

Heather said, "I'm a grown woman, and I can do what I want. So to protect myself, I rerouted

some funds. If your dad drops me, I won't have anything, and I think I've earned more than that."

I went over to the couch and sat down. The two of them kept going at each other, with Thorne now playing referee. I actually didn't care what they did. I didn't care how they handled things. The Heather I thought I knew wasn't the same lady at all, and my dad was so messed up, no talk I could give him would fix that.

"I want you out of my house now, Heather. We're through. You have no more access to any of my stuff. You're not president of the fan club, you're no longer running the foundation, you're out."

"But I thought you loved me." She switched from anger mode to desperation mode.

"I love not having you around. How about that? I thought we had something. If anybody needs to be compensated for the mess created by this relationship, it's me. The way I want to be paid back is for you to walk out of my life without expecting anything else."

"You're going to turn me in to the authorities? You're going to turn *me* in?"

"You should probably give back the money," Thorne said to Heather. "I'm sure if you do that, nobody's gonna press any charges."

She came toward me with a teary face. Though it hurt my heart, I turned away, got up from the couch, and walked toward my room. I didn't want to see her or my dad. My dreams of a stable family were destroyed, and honestly, they both were to blame.

Four hours later it was two o'clock in the afternoon, and I was heading to the school for a football meeting. Coach wanted us to review film, look at our game footage, and review and scout the team we were going to play next. I was sitting behind Emerson and Ryder. I'd never been a jealous or envious person, but at that moment, I wished I were one of them. They both lived with both of their parents, and today of all days, I wished I could say the same.

"Okay, so the special teams award goes to Emerson," Coach Swords announced. "Defensive player of the game goes to Ryder. Let's check out the highlights from offense to see who you guys think should win that award."

The last thing I wanted was for them to pick me. My moves were on point, but I didn't need any extra attention called to the fact that I was cheating. Steroids had gotten me buff and doing supernatural moves, and if the other players looked too hard, gave me too many accolades, the attention would cause problems.

"I think it should be Gage!" I yelled out.

Everybody turned around and stared at me. Gage's passes were pathetic. The fact that I caught them was a miracle in itself. But when I shouted out his name, I hadn't counted on it causing more controversy. Chaz, our other quarterback who should have been playing, turned his eyes my way.

I didn't realize Gage was sitting behind me until he leaned up in my ear and said, "Good thinking in saying it should be me. Smart move, Stone."

"Nah, my boy is just being modest. For sure it's Stone. Who catches passes like that?" Ryder said.

"Da brother's on 'roids," Chaz muttered.

Though Gage thought the same thing, because I supported him and because he hated

Chaz, he stood up on top of the chair and got buck.

Gage told him, "Just because you're sitting on the bench don't mean you gotta hate on him too."

"You ain't got no skills for me to hate on," Chaz said to him. "If we keep playing you, we ain't gonna make the playoffs."

Gage huffed, "Well, with me as quarterback, we've been winning."

"Not because of your playing," Chaz pointed out.

Gage didn't back down. "And not 'cause of yours either. You didn't even touch the field. You don't even need to turn your uniform in this week to get cleaned. You're the one hating."

As the two of them went back and forth, people started whispering to each other about my performance. I heard the word "steroids" more than once. I felt so uncomfortable, but I had to stay cool.

"Listen up, guys. Settle down!" Coach Swords said. "I don't need all the talk. Let's just vote. Everyone who thinks Gage should get the offensive player of the game award, raise your hand."

My hand was the only one that went up. Then I turned around and saw that Gage's hand was up too. But did voting for yourself count?

"Two votes, point taken," Coach said, trying not to laugh at Gage.

So I guess it did. Then he had to ask how many thought I should get it. People seemed hesitant to raise their hands.

"Ford also had a great game!" I yelled out. Ford was our running back.

Gage kicked my chair from behind. "Does he know too?" he said.

I rolled my eyes, needing the jerk to shut up. He didn't even have confirmation of my steroid use. Players started clapping for Ford. I felt relieved when Ford won.

When the meeting was over, Coach called me into his office. Coach Swords was real easy to talk to. Everyone on the team liked him, except for Ford. If Coach was dating my mom, I'd probably have issues with him too, though the two of them seemed to be working through those issues now that Ford knew Coach was serious about the relationship.

"Come on in, Stone. Have a seat."

There was no way I could admit that I'd taken any performance-enhancing drugs. If I did, Coach would have no choice but to kick me off the team. However, he knew my character. I wasn't a liar. I prayed that he wouldn't ask me the question directly because I didn't want to be forced into lying.

He studied me for a long moment, watching my mannerisms, giving me stern eye contact, and then shook his head as if he didn't know what to do with me. It was like he didn't want to ask the question for fear of the answer he might receive. I didn't want to push the issue, but I had to stand firm. I had to give him a reason to believe in me. I was never known to be a shaky, weak, or timid individual, and though I wasn't loud like Chaz, Gage, and Ryder, I wasn't passive like Emerson and Hagen either. With me, what you saw was what you got.

"Do you need to talk, son? Is everything all right?"

I almost laughed. I was happy Coach took that approach because on the inside, everything wasn't all right, and he was giving me an out.

"I'm dealing with some stuff, Coach, but it's going to be all right. I know what I gotta do."

"I hope you know what you gotta do because I count on you to follow all my rules. You're usually pretty low key, but lately your name's been swirling, and some of the accusations haven't been the best. You know what I'm saying?"

"Yes, sir, Coach," I answered quickly, truly knowing what he was saying.

"I need that squashed. I don't want to get into anything specific, but I just want to tell you I'm proud of your playing."

Inwardly I was saying, "Hold up, wait a minute, Coach. Don't give me any compliments, dang." I must have looked uncomfortable, because Coach continued.

"I just mean your performance in the last couple of games has been superior, and you know they've been pretty dramatically different. This whole off-season your work ethic has been stellar. You come in early and stay late. You grew in height, so naturally your body is ready to take it to the next level. You don't need to give it any help."

"I got you, Coach," I said. "And you have nothing to worry about."

"Well, that's all I needed to hear. Now get on out of here. And tell your dad that if his offer still stands, I would like to try to get two tickets to the concert Tuesday night."

"But, Coach, we got school Tuesday."

"First of all, I'm not a student. Second of all, it's a teachers' workday. That's why we practiced yesterday, remember? Students have no school Tuesday. I only have to be here in the morning, then I'm off."

"I didn't know you liked Sweet Lips' music."

"I like it okay, but as I'm sure you know, Ford's mom and I—"

"Yeah, yeah, yeah, I know about that," I teased as I jabbed him playfully in the arm. "You gonna pop the question anytime soon?"

"Hey now, you're the one that's supposed to be in the hot seat, not me," Coach protested, embarrassed. "But she's a fan, so—"

"My dad and I aren't really speaking right now, but I'll text him and give him your information. It should be no problem to get you on the list."

"I know your dad isn't around here all the time like most of the fathers, Stone," he said as he came around from behind his desk and put his hands on my shoulders. "But your father cares. He's giving so much to this program, a lot of which is anonymous. But I can tell it's him from the handwriting on the checks—it matches the writing on Sweet Lips' cardstock. I don't have a son, but I feel like I've got ninety young men. You teenagers are something else."

"It's not me, Coach. Trust me, it's not me."

"Well, us adults go through stuff too. Sometimes we need some grace. Anytime you want to share, I'm here. Everything will be all right."

"Good."

"I know you got it. You're one of the most responsible young men on this team. Remember, to whom much is given, much is required. You figure out what that means for you."

"I hear you. I gotta keep standing."

"Absolutely. And text me about those tickets."

"All right, Coach," I laughed and said as I went out of his office.

I didn't get two feet before I saw Ryder sitting there.

"We need to talk," he said.

"What's up?"

"No, not here. Not in front of Coach's door."

"All right." I grabbed my stuff, and we went out to his car.

"We still tight?" he asked.

"We cool."

He'd had a lot going on this semester. He started rubbing a lot of people the wrong way when he was dating Ariel Holiday. This wasn't the sixties. However, some people were still uneasy about interracial dating. It looked like he and Ariel had resolved to just be good friends, which was fine because both of them were players and not at all ready to settle down. I did think they were cute together, but I wasn't a matchmaker and certainly didn't care.

How cool were we? He hadn't come to me when he was having problems with that, and even worse, when he got into a big scandal that ended with a teacher getting fired and even arrested for having a relationship with him. I knew all that had to have been hard, but he hadn't confided in me, so I didn't know if we were cool or not.

"I need you to tell me the truth," he said slowly, his eyes searching my face. I could tell he was trying to gauge whether we were still boys like we were last year. "You taking something, man? If so, I can get you help."

At that point, I just lost it. When he put his hands on me, I flipped him off and said, "You know what? You take care of you. I got me. You said we were boys, and you're supposed to know me. Don't step to me with no crap. Lay off."

Very Damaged

When I arrived at school on Monday morning, I felt like a pariah. I usually hung with my football teammates, but they weren't standing in our normal spot by the door checking out all the honeys coming in.

It was an unspoken rule that whenever the group moved to another place and didn't tell one person, it was because that person wasn't invited to hang. I knew I probably should have opened up to Ryder just like I'd wanted him to open up to me when he was going through stuff. But I didn't know how to. How could I tell him all his assumptions about me using 'roids to get bigger, faster, and stronger were true?

I looked over his way, and although I could tell he was pissed at the way I ended our conversation, I needed him to believe in his boy.

So I walked over to him, held out my hand, and said, "I'm sorry about yesterday, man. I'm just stressed."

Finally he gave me dap. Before we released the handshake he pulled me a little closer and gave me a smile, which meant we were cool. Or maybe we weren't cool, because when our teammates surrounding him started getting antsy, looking at him funny, and finally walking away, he didn't say screw them. Nah, he gave me the brush off and walked away too.

Low as I felt, I perked up when I saw Victoria House walk past me. My feet started moving then. The way her hips were swinging locked my eyes in. For a moment, nothing else mattered but her. But she seemed more melancholy than usual. When I saw the gloomy look on her face, I wanted to reach out, put my arms around her, and tell her everything was going to be okay.

It was strange for me to feel this way. I didn't understand what was going on with me. I was always a ladies' man, with two, three, four girls

on my mind at a time. But for the last few weeks, Victoria House had me mesmerized. As soon as I was about to say something, I got a firm hit on the back. I turned and saw it was Emerson. Victoria, he, and I had the same lit class. The week before, the teacher had put us together to work on a group paper, and that day during class we had to fine-tune it together.

Emerson said, "What's going on with you, man? I wanted to talk to you after practice yesterday, but Coach called you into his office, so I kept it moving. I saw you weren't with your crew this morning. I'm not trying to get all in your business, but I'm here for you if you need me."

I did like the fact that Emerson was new on the team and wasn't a part of all the boy drama. He was a cool guy with a fresh perspective. The fact that his dad was a pastor made me hold Emerson up on a pedestal a little bit, truth be told. But I did need to talk to somebody before I popped. However, I had to be careful about what I said because I didn't want him to have a moral obligation to tell on me to Coach or anybody else.

I looked at him, shook my head, and said, "I can't talk to you. You got a mouth like a girl."

"Oh, stop. When have I ever told anybody someone else's business? You need someone to talk to, man. I'm here for real."

"You wouldn't understand. You don't have any issues. Your life's like a TV show, all perfect and everything."

"I don't know what TV shows you watch, but in every episode there are issues. Every family's got them. Mine is no different," Emerson boldly told me.

When we got into the classroom, Victoria said, "Let me just finish up the first draft—I was working on it at home. Then I'll show it to you guys for clean up."

"We can help," I said, not wanting her to feel like she had to carry all of the burden.

Victoria stood her ground. "I got the research you guys sent over, so let me do the part I said I would, and that's write the first draft. Then we can clean it up. You guys just work on the cover page."

Our literature teacher wanted everything to be nice, professional, and college ready. I pulled out my laptop and started fiddling with a cover image. Emerson took my computer from me when he saw I was distracted.

"Why don't you just talk to the girl?" he leaned in and said under his breath, like he knew what I was thinking.

Not denying his thoughts, but keeping it all in perspective, I whispered back, "Does she look like she wants anybody to talk to her?"

"From what her sister's said, she needs somebody. You always trying to act all hard like you don't care, but I know you do."

"Tell me about you. Make me feel better. Tell me your family's misery because I don't believe you have any problems."

"Being the pastor of a church is a lot. You got women who say they want prayer, but really they want intimacy."

"What?" I said, shocked at where I thought this was going.

"And even the most godly man can be tempted."

"Right, right," I uttered, knowing he had a point.

Emerson said, "Wrong, wrong."

"Nah, definitely wrong. I'm just saying I can imagine."

"Yeah. You can imagine a man unable to resist doing right," Emerson said in a disdainful tone.

Not sure where he was going with this, I said, "Well, I'm sure your dad resisted. One thing I've seen over the years is that Reverend Prince cares for his wife, unlike Lars Bush did his. My dad let my mother walk out, and he never went after her."

Emerson explained, "Just give him some slack. If it's stressing issues with your father, I can tell you parents can be so oblivious and naive to what's going on in their own world and definitely what's going on with their children. I thought my dad was having an affair. He thought I was crazy. My mom even accused him of it, but this is between me and you."

"Yeah, yeah, for sure," I said, truly in disbelief over the news.

Emerson continued, "He swore up and down the lady was on the up and up. But she was all over him. You see the picture?"

"Dang, that's crazy. I get what you're saying!"

"And it wasn't until my dad saw first-hand how inappropriate this lady was that he woke up. I don't know what it's going to take to make your dad wake up, but don't give up on him, man. That's all I'm saying." Emerson dropped

his voice again. "And what got me through my stuff was her sister," he nodded toward Victoria. "I ain't saying she's the girl for you, but I know there's some chemistry going on between the two of y'all. Maybe you want to check that out."

Seeing Victoria looking stressed and preoccupied, I said, "We're probably both too messed up to help each other."

He looked at Victoria again himself and obviously didn't see what I saw. "Now you're being naive. If you are right and you're both already broken, y'all can't hurt each other. Right?"

"Right," I said in a whisper as he turned the laptop back around, and I saw that the title page he created was really sweet.

Sweet as Victoria's lips that I wanted to kiss. But as soon as class was over, she jetted out of the door, and when I walked past her, hoping I could walk her to class, talk to her, say something, she turned the other way. She was clearly trying to tell me that I couldn't do anything for her but continue walking on. So that's what I did.

The school day was really getting long, and my temper was getting short. Not only did I

physically not feel good, I was starting to sweat profusely, and it wasn't even hot. I was finding it difficult to breathe. Also I was paranoid. It seemed everywhere I walked, people were staring at me, whispering about me. If I could just overhear one of them saying the wrong thing, I would make them wish they hadn't. Stepping into calculus class, I really became annoyed when our teacher, Ms. Rifle, said we had a quiz.

"How can we have a quiz? You haven't taught anything!" I went off on her.

Ms. Rifle snapped back and said, "Okay, then it's a pop quiz. Get out your pencil and paper, and let's go." Grumpily, I reached in my backpack to comply, but she stopped me. "Not you, Stone. You can grab a seat in the hallway for mouthing off."

Our principal, Mr. Fowler, walked down the hall a few minutes later, and he was displeased to find me in it instead of in class.

"Stone Bush, what are you doing out here, son? And don't tell me nothing, because teachers don't put you out in the hallway for nothing."

"Just got a little hot under the collar, sir. I don't know what's wrong with me."

"Well, the way you're playing ball, I know we need you on the field Friday night."

"Yeah, that's why I didn't get sent to the office. The teacher's trying to make sure she doesn't mess me up for football season."

"So you see, she's working with you. But you're not working with her!"

Dropping my head, I said, "Yeah, I've got to do better."

"So many young people think teachers are their worst enemies. Sometimes you got to look within and ask yourself, am I doing all that I can?"

"It's just a lot to manage, sir. It's not as easy as all that."

"I understand."

"No, we've got a pop quiz, and she hasn't even taught the material. I mean, who oversees the teachers to make sure what they're doing is right?"

"Well, there's a right way to state your grievance, and there's a wrong way to complain."

"I've been at this school for almost two and a half years, and I've never seen a kid's voice heard by the administration."

"Well, you've got to give me a chance to try. You do have a new math teacher, and this is a new curriculum. Though calculus class has been around a long time, they're mixing it with other things to comply with national standards. So I know the teachers are moving at an extremely accelerated pace to cover it all, and I don't have a problem examining their methods so that everybody wins and you guys master every part. Just come to me next time. Don't explode on the teacher."

I nodded and smiled. Mr. Fowler tapped my back to ensure me I could keep going. I felt like a weight had been lifted off of me. Finally I was getting someone to hear me out.

On my way to practice, I saw Victoria near the girls' locker room. She looked like a little girl who had lost her puppy, and deep inside my heart, I wanted to be the one that found it for her and made her smile again. I wondered why she was so glum. She'd been this way for a while. I remembered going to the restaurant after the football game and seeing Victoria with a long face.

I didn't know what was going on with her and the rest of the cheerleaders, but when Ariel and Yaris came out of the locker room and walked by her without even stopping, I realized there was some kind of beef. I wanted to reach out and comfort Victoria as she passed me. But I didn't. She made it blatantly clear before that she didn't need my help.

Actually, I understood how she felt when I opened up the locker room door a moment later and heard my name brought up in a not-so-flattering manner.

"Heck yeah, Stone's taking steroids. I don't need to bet you. I could definitely keep your money."

"It ain't like you got proof," another guy said.

"I seen him take them," a scrawny freshman lied and said.

"What?" a teammate shouted out in awe.

"Yeah, right after practice," the ninth grader kept adding to his story.

I didn't know who the little scrub was, but the voice sounded like freshman Will Johnson. He was absolutely lying. When I peeked around the corner, there he was with about ten other

guys around him listening intently. Then I saw Ryder in the pack.

Chaz asked, "Ryder, you know him, man. What you think?"

Ryder said, "I don't know."

"We saw you talking to him after the meeting yesterday."

I looked a little harder and saw Chaz all in Ryder's face trying to get him to speak against me. My blood was boiling as if it was being cooked on a stove top. Why couldn't they leave this alone?

Chaz pried, "What did he tell you when you asked him? Y'all supposed to be boys."

In a soft whisper, Ryder said, "He didn't answer."

Chaz scoffed, "That means he's taking 'roids. You know Stone. If he wasn't on anything, he'd be saying that he wasn't. We all know white boys can't jump like he's been jumping, and he got so much faster. What other explanation is there?"

Ryder seemed irritated. "I said I don't know."

Chaz pushed Ryder in the chest. "You need to quit being a punk and man up and say what you know to be true. Two plus two equals four.

There is no other way he could get as good as he's gotten unless he's doing something illegal to enhance his performance. Admit it."

"All right, I think you're right, dang."

I felt like a brick had just been dropped on top of my head. I had a pounding headache. I wanted to break something because it felt like my best friend was betraying me. Yeah, Ryder and I had drifted away from each other a little, but we'd always had each other's backs. We'd been playing football together through middle school and now high school—tight end going up against the middle linebacker—and for years we both played the same positions.

Coach came out of his office and yelled, "All right! Time to get ready for practice."

When the guys came around the corner to leave the locker room, Ryder and I came face-to-face. He could tell in my eyes that I was disappointed. He betrayed me, but the look he gave me back made me ashamed of myself. His eyes seemed to say, "Am I wrong?" I moved out of the way and let him exit.

When I was alone in the room, I banged my head repeatedly against one of the lockers.

Taking steroids was my own dumb choice. If I didn't want to have all this skepticism surrounding my play, I had to let the drugs go.

I knew taking them was wrong, so why was I getting frustrated that others questioned me? I guess I was growing up, though, because I felt like I was letting my whole team down. I wasn't blaming anybody but me. But I didn't feel good enough to play without the steroids and how they made me feel.

The rest of practice was a blur. I tried not to stand out or do anything spectacular. I didn't want anyone talking to me, not that any of them were heading my way to start a conversation anyway. Honestly, I wanted to quit, and in order for me to get to that place, I had to be real low because I was always a fighter. Now that I knew I couldn't conquer my fear, I realized I was a coward.

"What's going on with Victoria?" I asked as I saw her being escorted out of the gym by her mother.

She appeared to be in pain; her face held a look of agony. But I asked the wrong girl because Jillian had no sympathy.

"Just a little sprain. What do you care? Because I know if you aren't trying to get with this, you're not trying to get with that."

Jillian was still real salty that I turned her down, but she was extremely happy that she had something to shove in my face.

She continued, "You know, I'm glad I didn't let you have any of this. 'Cause word on the street is you got real problems. Looks like what I was attracted to was a facade."

"You should know fake people when you see them," I said before walking past her.

I was going to say something to Victoria. I really didn't care what was up any of the other cheerleaders' butts; her sister wasn't even trying to help her get to the car. But before I could get there, they took off. My phone started vibrating. It was my dad.

He said, "I'm headed out, son. Come on home; I want to talk to you about something."

It was time for his tour. The opening show was down in Savannah. What was it he wanted to talk to me about? As soon as I pulled up to the house, I saw my dad's tour bus in the driveway, loaded up and ready to leave.

Thorne stepped off it and said, "Your dad's been waiting on you. He really, really wants to talk to you. He's got one of his feelings."

One of his "feelings" meant that unless he made everything right in his world, his concert would go horribly wrong. Usually, when he held me tight or hugged me really hard when I was growing up, it wasn't because he loved me so much. It was because he didn't want to bring any bad omen on himself. He was such a superstitious rock star, and though the bus should have left already, he wasn't going anywhere until he felt all was well with his soul.

"Where is he, Thorne?" I questioned when I didn't see my father.

Thorne replied, "He's in the house getting one more bag."

"And you're not watching him? You don't know what he's doing!"

"We already talked about it. He's not bringing anything he doesn't need on this tour. You know what I'm saying."

"No, I don't, and you shouldn't believe him."

"It *is* taking him an awfully long time to go in there and come right out."

My dad was so good at hiding his stashes. He meant so much to me. As hard as I tried to pretend that I didn't need him in my life, my feelings showed as I dashed toward the house. He was my everything.

"Dad, where are you? Where are you?" I yelled out.

"You don't have to worry. He's fine. He's not getting drugs," Thorne said.

"Because you wish it were so doesn't make it that way, Thorne. Come on, man! This is my dad we're talking about. What tour has he been on that he hasn't brought a stash for?"

Thorne couldn't answer me. When my dad didn't answer either, I went to his special bathroom in the basement. I purposely didn't knock on the door. That would give him time to put away whatever it was he was doing. That would make me angry. I went to turn the doorknob, but it was locked.

"Dad. Let me in! Let me in!" I demanded.

Finally he responded, "I'm coming, son. I'm coming. I got to get on the bus. I … I been meaning to talk to you."

He was slurring his words, talking

irrationally. I knew he was taking something, and without even thinking, I used my shoulder to ram the door. It didn't open. I hit it twice; it still didn't open. Thorne helped me, and it opened. My dad was hastily stashing what looked to be drug paraphernalia.

"Okay, well, that's it. I wanted to have just a little edge. I'm a little nervous about the tour, son," my dad said, wiggling his body like he was a standing snake or something.

Making him stand still with my hands, I said, "Dad, are you serious? Why are you doing this? Your fans love you. You don't need an edge."

"I'm getting older, son. My vocal cords won't work the same if I don't feel confident."

"Dad, the concert is tomorrow. Why are you doing this now?"

"I've got some radio interviews to do on the way down there, and I just need to be my ol' Lars self, ya know? It was just a little something ..."

I looked at Thorne. We'd had an agreement. He was going to step in and help me make sure that my dad stayed clean.

"Lars," Thorne tried pitifully to intervene. "We got to get on the bus."

Angry, I said, "That's all you're going to say to my dad?"

"I'm grown. I pay his salary. Of course that's all he's going to say to me."

But I looked at my dad like, *Come on*. Then I looked hard at Thorne again.

"Are you going to let my dad talk to you like that? You care about him. You're not doing him any good by letting him ruin his life."

"Lars, man, we talked about you not getting high. You told me you didn't have anything. Where'd you get this?"

"This is all I have, goodness gracious."

My dad turned around and started looking for something.

Picking up on the fact that he was hiding something, I said, "What's wrong, Dad? What is it?"

"Um ... um, my suitcase. Is it on the bus?"

"Nah, you came back in to get it," Thorne said to him.

My dad seemed to suddenly realize where it was. He dashed out of the bathroom, and I ran after him.

"What's in the bag, Dad? What's in the suitcase? What is it you don't want me to find?"

"Nothing, nothing. I just … I just need to grab it so we can get out of here. I'm late."

Because he was stoned, I was able to sprint past him and grab the suitcase. But just as my fingers closed around the handle, my father yanked it from me. I jerked it back. We tugged on it until the thing opened.

It didn't contain any clothes—no underwear, toothbrush, deodorant, none of that. Its contents were pills, powders, and assorted drug paraphernalia. As the pills fell over the floor, my dad got down on his hands and knees, pathetically trying to grab each one. It was gut-wrenching. I caught him by the shoulders and shook him roughly.

"What are you doing? What is this all about? Why, Dad, why?" I was truly broken-hearted.

"Son, you don't understand. I need this, okay? I … I need this." I was seeing my dad as a completely different man. He was whining, crying, and pitiful. "Don't hit me, son. I need you to love me. Your dad's going to be okay. I'm just very damaged."

Dominant Presence

Okay. Fine, fine, fine," my dad surprised me by saying. "Clean up all of this. Flush it down the toilet, Stone. I'm fine. I don't need to have it. You're right."

"That's good you're gonna quit," Thorne stepped up to my dad and said. "But if you've been on something and I didn't know it, you're not going to be able to just go cold turkey. You're going to have to take something to straighten it out."

"I'll be fine," my dad said to Thorne before turning back to me. "Son, I don't want to

disappoint you, and I want to be around. Thorne told me you've been taking steroids."

Truly upset, like I'd been ratted out to the cops or something, I said, "What? You told my dad?"

Thorne explained, "Yeah, I was trying to get him to quit. I wanted him to know what a bad influence he has been."

"Thanks," I said, half meaning it.

My dad said, "I'm sorry, son. I'm sorry I've been a bad example. I love you. You know that, right?"

"Yeah, Dad. I love you too."

My dad gripped my shoulder. "You're always standing up for what you believe in, even if it's against your old man. You're not going to waver. And I don't know what made you feel like you're not big, fast, or strong enough, but you are. You don't need anything."

My dad and I hugged. It was the first time in a long time, and I really felt we connected. We both needed help, but maybe we could help each other.

"Since Mrs. Fernandez is here to watch the house, maybe you should come."

"Oh, Dad, I'm just going to chill. We don't have school or football practice tomorrow."

"I understand. We'll talk more when I get back."

"Yes, sir," I said, oddly not wanting him to leave.

"Come on and let your dad get on the road," Mrs. Rosa Fernandez, our housekeeper, said to me, picking up on my hesitance.

Her daughter Yaris was on the cheerleading squad. We really didn't talk much even though we ran in the same circles. I suspected Yaris was embarrassed that her mom worked for my father. I didn't know why. He paid good, and we loved her.

"*No estés triste*. Don't be sad. And don't look so grim, Stone," Rosa said to me. "Your father will be okay. I saw the way he looked at you. He's going to be fine this time. I'll clean all this up and discard it. You go on and eat and get to bed."

It wasn't that late, but Rosa knew me. I was tired. I ate her delicious meal and took a long shower. As I brushed my teeth, I looked at myself in the mirror and thought that this was a defining moment. I was telling my dad that he

could make it and get on stage and do his thing without any assistance. I had to believe I could do the same. I just didn't know why I wasn't sure, why I was reluctant, why I didn't want to let go of the crutch.

I opened the medicine cabinet and found the steroid pills. I only had two left. Just as I started to flush them down the toilet, I turned and put them back in the cabinet. I didn't take one, but I couldn't bring myself to completely destroy them either. I knew I was headed for trouble.

I was tired of not being able to get any sleep. I was tossing and turning. I didn't know if it was still the steroids in my system or if it was the fact that I was mentally drained, so fried that I really couldn't wind down. Whichever it was, I was irritable.

Then I started thinking about somebody just as bad off as me, and she was worse off because she was physically hurt. Victoria House came to mind. I looked at the clock and saw it was too late to call. Then I fell asleep.

When I woke up, I stared at the clock again. It was now too early to call Victoria. But I picked up the phone to call her anyway. Then I thought,

"Why would Victoria want to talk to me?" I realized I was a guy, but I didn't have to be so macho that I let it keep me from telling her how I felt about her. Maybe if she knew I cared, she'd open the steel door she had barricading our friendship and let me in so we could explore all that my mind was dreaming of. Finally, I worked up the nerve to call her.

Five minutes into the conversation, I was shocked when she just out of the blue asked me if I was going to my dad's concert. I hadn't even realized she'd been listening to me and Emerson talk about it at school, but I guess she had. When she said she'd go, I figured I could kill two birds with one stone, no pun intended. I could be there for my dad and be with her at the same time.

What was it about Victoria House that I liked? Everything: her naturally tawny skin, her gorgeous copper eyes, the boldness in her voice, her walk, her beautiful little body. It took me less than an hour to get over to her house to pick her up. Then we were heading down to Savannah.

When she batted her eyelashes my way, I wanted to break the silence. As much as I told myself it was time to man up and state my

feelings, I felt like a nerdy, shy little sixth grader unable to find the right words. Never had my heart beat so strongly for a girl. Though I knew she wasn't fragile, I could tell she was in a vulnerable place.

"You're beautiful," I said as I stroked her brow.

"What are you talking about?" she said as if I was lying.

"What? You don't think you are?"

"Uh, no. I'm actually surprised you want me to tag along. I thought you would want to ask Jillian or somebody like that."

"Are you serious? Please. She wishes."

"I didn't think it was one-sided when I saw the two of you interact."

"No, Victoria, I've been making eyes at you, and I thought there was something between us, but uh—"

"Oh, I like this song!" she said as Sweet Lips' new hit came on the radio.

She reached to turn it up, and I did at the same time. When our hands touched, I took my fingers and let them slide between each of hers. Gently I squeezed her hand, and when she

turned and smiled at me, we connected in a special way. When we got to the other side of Macon, I pulled over to get gas and something to eat.

"I told your mom I was going to take care of you. You have to order something," I said, disappointed when she said she didn't want anything.

She didn't actually say that she was watching her weight; however, I could tell that's what it was. She looked down at her stomach, then turned her face away from me toward the window like she was ashamed. Of what, I don't know. Girls were weird that way.

In the most sincere voice I could muster, I said, "I'm not going to force you to eat, but you're perfect just the way you are."

"You're just saying that," she said to me.

As I tried to convince her she was fine, I knew I was also talking to myself. I so wanted to open up to her to let her know my own struggles with my body, but I didn't. I couldn't. So I said nothing.

When we got back on the interstate and were once again heading toward our destination, we talked about everything else. We talked about our favorite TV shows. Mine was *CSI*, and

hers was *The Real Housewives of Atlanta*. When she admitted to that, we both laughed. Next we joked around, and I asked her what position she would play if she were a football player. I chuckled just imagining her dressed in the uniform. Her response was too cute.

"I'd be the kicker," she answered me, real sure of herself.

"You'd be the kicker, huh?" I said.

"Yeah, I don't want to get hit. I'd just kick the ball through the H-double-O-P."

"That's basketball."

"I know. I'm playing with ya. Plus, I need to get ready to cheer for my favorite sport. Y'all need to hurry up and finish the season."

I smiled. I was ready for football to be over too. It was crazy cool being with her, just as I thought it would be. Talking to her was real relaxing—not stressful at all.

When we got to the hotel, I saw my dad's tour bus. I knew the concert wasn't going to start for another couple of hours, and I was actually excited to see him. I wanted him to be happy I was there. I truly hoped he hadn't gotten with any of his band members and gone back on his word.

Like normal, Thorne was stationed outside of his door. But he didn't look too happy to see me, and he wasn't letting Victoria in until I cleared it with my dad. I was embarrassed when I found my dad was walking around his suite naked.

"What are you doing here?"

"I came to see you, Dad. What are you doing?"

"I know it looks a little weird, but I'm developing a new ritual. If I can't get high, I can let it fly."

"What do you mean, Dad? You're not Superman. Plus, I got company."

"Who?"

"It's this girl, Victoria."

"You didn't have to bring somebody hours down the road. If you wanted to come, you should've got on the tour bus. It's dangerous, son. I didn't even know you were traveling."

"It was spur of the moment. Are you okay?"

My dad walked to the bedroom, got his favorite robe, and thankfully, put it on. He said, "I am, and with you here I'm sure I won't be going off the straight and narrow. Come over here, boy."

He put me in a headlock like he used to do when I was ten. Though I was bigger than him and much too old for the childish maneuver, I didn't put up a fuss. My dad and I were bonding.

As he let me back up he said, "Now, where is this girl of yours? She better be hot."

I gave him a smile, and when Thorne let her in, my dad gave me a subtle nod of approval. Victoria was hot all right.

It didn't take long for my dad's entire entourage to show up, including a logistics team.

"Sir, we have a little crisis brewing," a serious-looking lady from the team said to my dad.

"What do you mean?"

"A storm is supposed to come through here tonight around midnight. I'm only telling you because storms are unpredictable, and it could come earlier. It's not even supposed to hit this particular area badly, but that could always change. We're just checking because we wanted you to be aware in the event that you want to cancel."

"No, no, no, we can't cancel," a shady-looking man interjected. "This show's been sold out for months. I've been checking the weather, and it's

under control. I didn't even want to bother you with this. We're going to be fine."

"A storm? Tonight?" I said to Thorne in a low voice.

"Yeah, sounds like it's not going to hit where we are, but I'd just rather your father be safe than sorry. They're pushing him to go on with this concert. You know how people are when they want to maximize money. It's sold out so they don't want him to back out."

"Right, right."

"But if anything goes wrong, they're going to be looking at him, asking why he didn't cancel."

Giving him a worried glance, I said, "You said the storm wasn't going to hit here."

"Nah, but storms can take funny turns."

"Can you get my dad's attention? He usually listens to you."

"The band's all pumped. Everybody needs money when you're not on tour. The cash flow gets tight. There's a lot of pressure on him to keep it going, so y'all need to come on so we can get this thing moving and have it behind us."

My dad had to go meet with his band. Everyone emptied out of the room, leaving Victoria

and me alone. I forgot about the storm for the time being.

We started making out on a couch in a bedroom sitting area. I wanted to seduce her, but she was shaking.

I pulled her close to me and asked, "What's wrong?"

"You're making me nervous," she said, shaking like the leaves of a tree in the wind.

"I don't mean to."

She felt my muscles, and then she touched my chest. "You're so strong."

And then she looked down, and I couldn't hide my excitement.

She blushed and turned away, but I held her from the back and kissed her neck. Hurting her was the absolute last thing on my mind, and I didn't want it to be something she was concentrating on either.

Seeming overwhelmed, she exhaled. "Why do you like me? Why do you want to be with me?"

I whipped her around toward me and kissed her like I'd never get another kiss in my life.

She softened and smiled.

"Are you ticklish?"

"What are you doing to me?" she moaned. "I just want us to talk. This moment is too special to rush. I've liked you for a while, Stone, and to think you like me too is … I don't even have the words."

"Well, how about I play with your feet?"

I took off her socks, revealing perfectly painted red toenails on dainty, delicate, precious feet. I kissed one toe and then another.

"I mean it!" she squealed as she jerked her feet away. "Let's just be calm."

"How's your other foot doing?" I asked, trying to change the subject.

I touched it gently and saw it was still a little swollen. I grabbed a pillow and propped up her injured foot.

"Oh, thank you, Stone. I'm fine, though."

"Yes, you are," I said slowly as my lips made their way to hers, and they did their own dance for about three minutes.

The warmth I was feeling from our bodies pressing against one another was just the tip of the iceberg compared to the way I suspected she could really make me feel. When we heard

someone fidgeting with the door, I got up and told her I'd be back.

Victoria said she was gonna freshen up. "But I enjoyed our time." She blew me a kiss.

Before I could answer the door, Thorne came in and went into my dad's room in search of something. I turned on the TV and flipped through the channels until I found the weather. I was shocked when they said Savannah was under a storm watch.

"Dang, it's a storm watch now? It was just a severe thunder storm twenty minutes ago."

"Get your girl, and let's go," Thorne said, coming out of my dad's bedroom. "We need to get over to the concert center."

"But look, they're saying all the severe weather is just south of us."

"Still, I'm nervous," Thorne said.

"I'm ready," Victoria announced as she came out from the bedroom smiling from ear to ear.

She had put on a different sweater—a cute, cream-colored fitted one. She'd also changed into tight jeans that were hugging her in all the right places. She had on some long black boots that made her really look sexy.

Thorne saw me go all goo-goo eyed, so he said, "I'm serious, Stone. Y'all need to come on down. You guys have to ride with us in the limo in order to get back stage. We need to roll on out. Here are your passes."

He handed us lanyards, one of which I slipped around Victoria's neck.

"Let's go," Thorne said when he thought I was taking too long.

He went out the door without acknowledging Victoria. Uneasy, Victoria pulled my shirt and said, "He doesn't like me very much."

I turned to her and said, "You're with me; he likes you. He's just uptight and definitely not in as good of a mood as I am 'cause he doesn't have you like I do."

"Stop it," she said.

"I told y'all to come on!" Thorne said in such a strong, stern voice that both of us hopped to it and were on our way.

Pulling up at the concert actually gave me a newfound appreciation for my father. Fans were screaming as they lined the ropes on both sides of the entranceway. People considered him royalty.

Victoria was giddy. "I can't believe I'm in your father's limo following the Sweet Lips tour bus. If my mom knew, she would freak, punch me out, and immediately take my place."

"You think she likes my dad's music that much?"

"Yeah, she's way crazy about it."

"You want something to drink?" I said, remembering being in the limo when I was younger and checking out the stored beverages to help myself to pop and bottled water.

"No, I'm okay," she voiced bashfully.

"You know you got me worried about you. You're not eating."

"Okay, don't make a big deal of it," she said, her mood changing real quick. She was getting a little frustrated with me.

I put my hands up in the air. "Sorry."

"No, I'm sorry. I wasn't trying to bite your head off. I'm just dealing with some stuff."

She didn't have to tell me, I was dealing with my own drama; trying to figure out whether or not I was going to leave steroids alone, saying in my head that I was, but knowing that my muscles had a mind of their own, and they didn't want to get smaller.

My phone started vibrating. I pulled it out of my pocket and saw that I had a text from Ryder.

The text read: "Hey man. Just wanted to let you know you're my boy, and I ain't saying that I'm perfect either. I don't want you to admit anything to me, but word is Coach Swords is gonna press you to do a drug test when we go back to practice tomorrow. Take the information however you need to."

At that moment I couldn't respond to him. I didn't know what to say back, but I did need to know that information because he was dead on.

"Are you okay?" Victoria asked, sensing I was frustrated. "I do apologize. I didn't mean to—"

"No, no, it's not you. You're just not the only one with problems. That's all."

I could tell we really wanted to be there for each other and be transparent and share our issues. But something, maybe fear, was holding us back.

"We should just cancel it then," my dad said into his phone from the back of the limo.

"Everything okay?" Victoria whispered as she grabbed onto my arm, obviously a little worried.

"I hope so. There's supposed to be some rain."

"Uh, at an outdoor concert? That'll be yucky."

"I know, right? It might get pretty heavy. It looks like it's a mess as to what to do."

My dad hit the limo's window. "All right, fine, but if it gets too windy and if the warning goes up to a watch, I'm cutting the concert short."

When we pulled into the backstage area, it was time to unload the limo and tour buses. I knew Victoria didn't want to go anywhere without me, but I needed to talk to my dad real fast in private. As more people surrounded him, trying to go over last minute performance details, he waved at me and shooed me on, basically telling me "Don't wait around." He gave me a thumbs-up, and that was his way of telling me he was happy I was there. I lifted my hand in the air too, nodded, and felt okay that he was okay.

As soon as I stepped out of the limo, I looked up to the sky. There wasn't a cloud to be found, but it was getting dark, and with daylight savings over, I passed it off on the time changing.

The one good thing about coming with the band was that there wasn't that much time between our arrival and my dad's actual performance. Since on

this tour Sweet Lips was the only big artist, local bands went on before him to warm up the crowd.

"Do you want to watch the show from backstage or do you want to go out front?" I asked Victoria.

I was really tripping that I was being such a gentleman. Whatever she wanted to do and what worked for her, I was for. That had never happened to me. Girls I'd been with, I didn't want to bend over backward to please, but in this case, I did. I really didn't want to do anything wrong. I wanted Victoria to know I truly cared about her feelings and that I could be the gentleman that she was looking for. The fact that my heart was softened somewhat meant I had chosen the right girl to care so deeply about.

She looked at me, batted her pretty eyelashes, and said, "Whichever you want to do is fine."

Boy, were we connected. The night was so lovely. Therefore, I figured if I went out to the blowing wind, she'd have to hold on to me tighter.

So selfishly, I said, "Let's check out the show from the front."

"But we won't have a good seat."

"Yeah, Thorne will have somebody take us out. We'll have to stand, though."

"That's great. I can get some pictures on my phone to send to my mom. She'll feel like it's an early Christmas present or something."

"I can get an autographed picture for her or something, or better yet, my dad can meet her when we get back."

"Oh my gosh, she'd love that."

One of the local security guys took us out right below the stage. Victoria was normally so laid back and reserved that I was excited to see her fired up. I made a mental note to give my dad props. She wasn't the only teenage girl out there screaming when the announcer let everyone know he was coming out, asking us if we were ready.

He might not have been an outstanding preacher like Emerson's dad, or as responsible as Ryder's father, but at least he was there and hadn't abandoned me like Hagen's and Ford's dads. My mom fled instead. I really appreciated my dad for doing the best he could and for actually making me proud. There had to be at least five thousand people there. Two thousand or so

pushing, trying to get even closer to the stage, and that was awesome.

I didn't give him enough credit for all the good that he did. I thought the crowd was loud already, but when he came out on stage, it got even louder. I was mad at him for not coming to my football games, but I realized it had been a long time since I went to one of his shows. Though this was his new fall tour, he'd had a few concerts in the spring and summer that I hadn't attended.

"I just want to say thank you that you guys came out to support me and Sweet Lips. I'm Lars Bush. I'm real proud today because I got my son in the audience. Where my young ladies at? Well, I would say, if you think I'm something, wait until you get a load of him, but he's actually with a honey tonight, so you'll just have to scream for me."

The girl to the left of me was with a guy in uniform, and she was cheering loudly. A larger lady right behind me was screaming like she was in a horror flick. Victoria looked up at me and blushed. I couldn't believe he acknowledged me. It was cool. What blew me away and made

me shiver even more were the next words out of his mouth.

"You know, my son is a football player, and I don't even get a chance to go see him play that often. But I think about him all the time, and I wrote him this song to tell him I'm proud that he's my boy. Y'all don't mind me starting out with something new, do you?"

The crowd screamed even louder, ready to hear him sing. He knew the answer was no, nobody minded.

"Your dad wrote you a song? That's awesome!" Victoria said to me.

The notes of the song were so beautiful. They were just as beautiful as the girl who was wrapped in my arms. The night was so perfect.

I looked up to say a little prayer of thanks. But as soon as I did, I saw a bolt of lightning hit so close that it scared me. It was like the sky broke through. The wind went from refreshing to horrifying as it picked up. The stage started shaking.

Instinctively, I grabbed on to Victoria tighter. People began to panic, and my dad's worst fear came true. The storm had turned, and we were

right in the middle of it. People started running to and fro. I saw a larger lady who needed help. Victoria needed to be safe, but this lady was in immediate danger. The stage was collapsing, and I was scared for the people closest to it. I yelled out to her.

"Go to safety! Go! I'll be okay."

As the steel structure was falling down on top of me, I heard her say, "What about you?"

I tried to hold up the stage. At first push, I was successful. Though I hadn't taken steroids that day, my natural adrenaline seemed to be kicking in. But when it buckled on top of me, it was way heavier than I'd anticipated. I realized I was no match for the storm's dominant presence.

CHAPTER SIX

Completely Exposed

Oh my goodness, it's coming down on me! Oh my gosh, help!" the large woman in her mid-thirties yelled out. I remembered seeing her earlier.

The stage had already come down on me, but a boulder, stick, brick, or something was still holding it up. There were steel bars holding up some of the unsteady stage. I was able to help the lady so that it didn't hit her in the head. At the same time, I didn't need it to crush either of us.

There were other people pinned as well, and we were on our knees. Because of the howling wind, relentless rain, and dark clouds, it seemed

like the dead of night. It was hard to focus. Then the lightning struck again, and I could see a hole toward the back of the stage. It seemed pretty big. We just had to maneuver our way back there.

A couple I'd recalled seeing earlier was under the structure too. Both the man and woman looked to be in their twenties. The guy was in a service uniform. "You see that too?" he asked me.

"Yeah," I told him. "We've got to help the ladies get out."

"Yeah. My girlfriend is scared to pieces," the guy said. "I'm Jim, and this is Kristy."

"Cool, I'm Stone."

We couldn't shake hands because we were all on our hands and knees. I said I'd take the front, and he took the rear. The lady in her thirties was huffing and puffing, breathing really hard. I hoped she could make it.

Needing to encourage her, I said, "Follow me. The couple will be right behind you."

The exit I'd spotted was at the back right corner. Every move I made toward the opening, it seemed to get further and further away. I realized we had to go to the left to get out because

the right side was completely crushed toward the front.

The lady behind me yelled out, "I can't do this."

"Yes, you can. Tell me your name," I said as I kept crawling forward.

In a panicked voice, she squealed, "Sarah."

"Okay, Sarah, stay focused, stay with me. We're going to make it out of this, but you've got to keep going. You've got to keep moving. You've got to stay positive."

"I'm just so tired and weak." The structure started shaking. "Can't you see it's about to come down on our heads? We're not going to make it out of here. Oh my gosh! Look out for the beams."

"Thank you," I said as I avoided the debris. "We've got to go faster."

Sarah stopped crawling. "What's that?"

Trying not to lose it, I calmly said, "It's nothing. Come on."

"No, no, it's somebody's arm. Oh my gosh!"

I turned around. The arm belonged to a young woman in her twenties. Jim checked for a pulse. When he looked grim and shook his head, I knew there was none. Kristy began to cry.

"Oh no, she's dead!" Sarah shouted.

I had been the one moving everyone along to get out of danger, but after seeing the body I could not move one inch. A lady who'd come to see my father perform had lost her life. It could've easily been me in her place. Then I realized if I didn't hurry up and keep it moving, it could still be me. And not only me, but me plus three others. I had to do everything in my power to not let that happen. Sarah and Kristy were rightfully devastated.

When Sarah wouldn't move, I asked, "Do you have kids?"

"Yes, I have two boys," she answered, sniffling.

"Take it from a guy whose mom hasn't been around. They need you. You got to keep going for them. We got to get out of here so we don't end up like this lady you just saw."

"I can't. I can't move. I can't go."

"If you think that your sons don't need you, then you stay right here."

"They need me! They need me!" she said.

"Then you've got to keep moving! Come on, you can do this!"

"But I'm so tired!"

The wind howled even more, and we heard louder screams. Jim said, "It's about to completely collapse. Y'all got to go, or we're going around you!"

Staring hard at Sarah, I shouted, "Come on, you've got to do it! You've got to go now!"

"Okay, okay, go, go," Sarah said as she hit me like I was the hold up.

We started booking it. As soon as we got almost to the clearing, more debris and steel beams from the stage came down, blocking our path. We couldn't turn around and go another way because the stage had collapsed. We found a little pocket of safety, but we were afraid if we moved any, the space above us would crumble like building blocks.

"We're going to die," Kristy said to Jim.

Sarah started praying. I looked at Jim. He looked at me. In our gaze we confirmed to each other that we had to stand firm and be strong for the ladies. We made a silent vow to figure this out.

However, just as soon as we'd decided to be resolute and unafraid, the safe space we were in

began to condense. Things tightened around us. It was like we were in a tepee with no slit in it to get out.

"I'm claustrophobic," Sarah shouted, appealing for me to do something.

"So we got to hurry up and get out of here. We can do this!" I said, not knowing whether this was indeed true or how we would accomplish it, but truly believing it.

Though I hoped my life was not about to end, I was a realist, and I had to admit that maybe this was it. The storm wasn't letting up. It was pushing everything down on top of us. We were in dire straights. I just took a moment to block out everything—all the noise, all the fear, and all the thoughts that my life was over. I hated that I hadn't taken a real chance on myself and believed that I could be my best without steroids. Yes, I liked the quick fix that they gave me: the edge, the speed, the dominance. But if I trained, if I worked hard, if I didn't give up, if I didn't quit, I could probably—no, definitely—do it on my own.

Unfortunately, I knew now I might not get the chance. But I smiled, realizing that I had stepped up on some things. I had tried to get

some things worked out in my life, tried to be a man and quit reacting off of emotions about everything. I wanted to be with Victoria. I'd just shared a special day with her. Yeah, we'd held each other. We'd connected, and it had felt good. I also had drama with my dad. It wasn't completely squashed, but he wanted me to be here. If I had to go out now, at least I would go out supporting him.

I hated that I hadn't texted Ryder back earlier. It had been cool of him to message me about the drug test. We'd always been straight with one another before. I hadn't been able to admit my weaknesses to him, but he let me know we were still cool anyway. The lightning struck again. I had to find a way to get out of there because I wanted to hug Victoria one more time. I wanted to tell my dad how much I loved him. I wanted to make things right with my teammates and win the right way.

I searched all around. To my left, directly opposite of where the hole had been, there were a bunch of bars. There was a small opening underneath them. If I dug a little in the dirt, I could crawl under it.

Jim helped me dig, and the ladies pitched in too. We didn't have much time, but I was certainly willing to try. I could do this—I had to. But as soon as I went under the bars, the structure gave out some more, pressing them down on me. I was trapped.

With all the strength I could muster, I forced myself to keep it together. It didn't look good, but I thought about my dad and Victoria. What if they needed me? How could I help them if I gave up? So though I was getting weak, I told myself that I was strong, that I could do it, and that I couldn't stop. I saw the emblem on Jim's uniform, and that also gave me courage.

I yelled out to him, "Hey, Marine, we're going to make it out of here, right?"

"That's right!" Jim replied with conviction.

I asked, "Can you help the ladies dig just a little? I'm going to squeeze on out."

He didn't even answer. He just started digging. Kristy and Sarah joined in. As I felt more space open up around me, I started rolling to the left and the right. I moved my body forward until I was free. Wreckage on top of my head started falling as well, and I knew I didn't have much time

before the whole structure completely collapsed. I started digging from the outside, making the hole that I'd just come through a little bit bigger.

"You got to come next," I said to Sarah.

Hesitantly she wailed, "No, I can't make it through that."

"Okay, well, I'm going to go through and pull you," the guy's girlfriend said. With ease, Kristy made her way through.

Sarah cried, "I can't do it."

Jim firmly told her, "You've got to do it. I'm going to push you through this end; they're going to pull you. You're going to get through. We've got to get out of here."

As the structure gave some more, closing in on us, we knew we didn't have much time. I told her to think of her sons, and she got in that hole and made dust go up in the air. She pulled herself through as hard as she could. We pulled, Jim pushed, and Sarah popped through. Kristy and I fell backward when she was through.

The marine went last and hauled himself through the hole like a pro. He actually crawled around us and led us to the opening. The four of us were out. Though we were covered in mud

and dirt, we'd survived. A chaotic scene greeted us: people were still running around panicked, sirens were going off, and the storm was raging on. But none of that really bothered me because we'd gotten free.

"I'll never forget you. I can't thank you enough. It's awesome we made it," Sarah said as she hugged me real tight.

I also got a pat on the back from the marine and a kiss on the cheek from his girlfriend. He said, "Stone, you could fight alongside me in battle any day."

"Thanks, man," I told him.

I saw my dad and Thorne and some of the other band members, including Bishop. My heart wanted to leap in their direction, but my legs stayed put. I was scratched up and beat down.

I had to blink my eyes a few times as I tried to comprehend the fact that Bishop was running my way. "Oh my gosh! Stone, is that you? Is that you?"

With our history, I couldn't understand why he seemed so happy to see me. He was wiping the mud off my face as if he were my mother or something. So much affection coming from my

nemesis was scary. But I guess when it got down to it, Bishop really was like family and would have been hurt if I was gone.

"Yeah, it's me. I'm okay. It's me."

"Oh my gosh, you're Bishop Warner!" Sarah jumped in front of me and said with glee.

Bishop saw all four of us covered in mud from head to toe, and said, "Yep, I'm Bishop. But forget me. Are you guys okay?"

I nodded. Sarah looked like she wanted to kiss him. Kristy was grinning wider than an ocean spans the globe.

Bishop looked back from where he'd come, saw my dad still panicked, and yelled, "Lars! He's over here!"

"I know he's not calling Lars Bush this way!" Kristy said, practically yanking Jim's arm off in her excitement.

My dad spotted Bishop and threw his hands in the air in a gesture of despair. He didn't recognize me, covered in mud as I was. Bishop clung to my shirt collar and pointed wildly at me. When my dad finally got the message, he came running. Both ladies screamed as their star came up close and personal.

"He's okay," Bishop said, seeing my dad's concern over my appearance. "Your son is okay."

"Your son?!" Sarah whacked me on the arm.

"Hey!" I said, indignant. Then I realized I hadn't told them who I was. It had been the last thing on my mind when we were trapped down there.

"Dad, I'm fine," I said, trying to reassure him.

My father said, "You had me worried. You look like crap, but you're in one piece. You're okay?"

"Yeah, Dad, but we saw some gruesome stuff down there."

"Some fatalities have been reported," he gravely acknowledged. I wondered how many more there were in addition to the unfortunate lady we'd seen.

"We need to have the fire department comb underneath there because we were pinned, and there could be other people stuck too," I told my dad urgently.

Just as I said that, the stage collapsed completely, flattening like a pancake. My dad just grabbed me, and he couldn't hold back the tears.

"You're okay. You're okay. You're okay," he kept repeating.

"I'm okay too," Sarah said.

My dad and I both realized we couldn't have a private moment right then. He motioned for an introduction. I obliged and introduced my dad to all three of them.

"Thank you guys for helping my son get out okay," my dad said with teary eyes.

Jim stepped up and said, "No, sir. Your son helped us. I'm a marine, but he was the cool, calm, and collected one. He kept his head. He saw us through. You should be proud."

My dad put my head in a lock. "I'm so glad that y'all are out and okay. You are okay, right?"

"Yes, sir, we're all okay," Jim replied.

The ladies didn't have purses or cell phones or anything to be able to pass on information to me so that I could make sure we stayed in touch. However, my dad did tell them where we were staying and invited them to come to the hotel suite later on that evening if they were still in town. Paramedics came over to us and wanted to check us out. Cops came over and talked to the marine to get his story. Immediately, volunteers

and other people started moving debris just to make sure there was no one else underneath still alive.

As my dad walked me up to a big hangar, he said, "I thought you were gone."

"I thought I was too, Dad, honestly."

"I love you, son."

And we just hugged real tight.

"I'm going to do better by you. I am," he uttered.

"Wait, Dad, where's Victoria? Oh my gosh, have you seen her?"

It wasn't like I'd forgotten about her. It was just my dad seeing that I was okay, all that had to be taken care of. Now that the formality was out of the way and he knew I was fine, I had to find her.

"Wait, son, just calm down. I'm taking you to her now," my dad said. He led me to the hangar ahead of us.

Once we were inside, he stepped back. I saw what looked like a beautiful angel. She was perfect, completely unharmed and in the midst of chaos she was a flower making my day bright. She hugged me.

"I thought I'd never see you again," she said as I wiped the tears from her beautiful face even though my hands were dirty.

"I'm sorry. I'm getting you all muddy."

"The fact that you're here before me … you could dunk me in a tub of mud, and I'd be okay. Just seeing you makes my day."

We weren't boyfriend and girlfriend. We hadn't even been good friends like we were now for that long. None of that mattered. We survived a tragedy, and in the embrace, we both got stronger.

"Nine people dead! Are you serious?" my dad said in despair to a room full of managers, concert promoters, and other people involved with the tour.

My dad's eyes filled up and rightfully so. It wasn't just nine bodies. Those were people who, because of his concert and the horrible events that happened there, would never be able to go home to their families, hug their children, kiss their wives, and live their lives. He'd forever be criticized for going on with the concert despite the weather report.

Boxer, my dad's manager, said, "You need to give some type of statement. Members of the media are standing out there. You got to say something, Lars."

My dad responded, "I don't want to say anything right now! I'm just a musician. I don't have any answers as to why this happened!"

Thorne and I could see my dad was clearly frustrated. And having to fight for my own life, not knowing if I was even going to make it, I realized I needed to stand up, grow a backbone, and be a man. It was like during a football game. Adversity may come, you may be down tons of points, but as long as there's time on the clock, you got to keep working, you got to keep trying, you got to keep pushing on toward the goal of winning. So I couldn't let my dad wallow in his despair. He hit the table, got up, and abruptly walked out of the conference room. I followed.

"Dad, it's going to be okay," I said.

"How's it gonna be okay, son?" he said. "How am I supposed to look at those people's families and tell them it's okay? I was almost in the same situation. I didn't think you were going to make it out of there. It's not fair that my son did and

their loved ones didn't. I mean, it's horrible of me to say, but this all seems like it's on me."

"Dad, none of us know when our last breath is going to be on this earth. We can only hope we go doing what we love. I found peace when that stage was coming down around me. I thought I wasn't going to get out. Part of me thought I should have stayed home and not come at all. But a bigger part of me wanted to be here to mend our relationship and get things right." I choked back some tears. "And in their last moments, hopefully those people who died were having fun, screaming and yelling at a concert. Sure we can analyze this, over analyze it if we want to know the truth and wonder why. But in those folks' last minutes, you provided happiness."

My dad reached out and hugged me real tight, like he was never going to let go. It was a weird exchange. The two of us knew we had a lot to deal with, but we'd been given more time, and I didn't want to waste it.

"So, Dad, you're going to go in there and give a statement. You don't have to have the right words. Just speak from your heart, and it will help people get through this tragedy."

"Look at this. My son is being a father. I'm going to do better, son. I promise. One thing I know is I can't keep doing these drugs."

"Me either, Dad."

"You don't need them."

"Somewhere inside I told myself that I did, but I know I don't. If we got to go to rehab together, if we have to be each other's accountability partners on this whole thing, we just got to do it, Dad. I'm serious!"

"All right, son. I hear you."

When my dad went in to give some words, I saw Victoria's smiling face. I went over to her, and she held her hand out. The two of us went up to my dad's suite. I sort of wanted us to pick up where we left off earlier before the concert. Hug, kiss, and make all our problems disappear. But now wasn't the time. As we rode up in the elevator without saying a word, we both knew now was the time for us to truly draw closer by sharing the painful issues that were tearing our individual worlds apart.

"I just feel like if I tell you what's going on with me, you won't like me anymore," Victoria said. She couldn't even face me.

Gently, I placed my hands on her shoulders and turned her around to face me. I drew her chin up so our eyes met, and said, "Ditto. But if you won't walk away from me, I'll be here for you."

"You say that now, Stone."

"Just give me a chance."

When we sat down on the couch in the penthouse suite, both of us were apprehensive. One thing about revealing too much of yourself to another person is you can never take back what you said. Trusting another teenager was always a gamble. But as I looked at the beautiful girl sitting next to me, I realized it was a risk I wanted to take.

But before I could speak, she shared some pretty personal stuff.

"So you know how the game last weekend was like my best one ever?" I said after she'd finished.

Trying to figure out where I was going, she hesitantly nodded. "Yeah, everybody's saying that because you caught that amazing pass, we were able to get in position to make the field goal."

"Have you heard anything else about my performance?"

"No. I don't know if you've noticed, but I've been kind of a loner lately."

"Well, word's been going around that I had help ... that I'm on steroids."

Looking appalled, Victoria said, "The people saying that are wrong, right?"

The fact that she thought there was no way I would use performance-enhancing drugs got to me. This girl believed in me, and now I was going to let her down. Extremely frustrated, I got up from the couch. Maybe opening up wasn't a good idea after all. I ran my fingers through my hair, feeling the weight of the world on my shoulders.

"Talk to me, Stone. Are you taking something?"

I just nodded my head.

"But I'm done with that. I swear. After tonight, I don't want to live a lie. I'm a good athlete. Yeah, sure I wanted an edge, but I can do this the right way."

"Gosh, I guess we have more in common than I thought."

I was happy to see her smiling. Our subject

matter was serious. After the horrible events we'd just been through, we needed our burdens lightened.

"You're beautiful, you know. You don't need to do anything crazy to your body to be thinner than you already are."

"I don't think I'm beautiful. I think I'm fat and overweight."

"No, no, stop. Don't even say that. You're perfect. You're tiny!"

I could tell she didn't know how to accept my compliments, so I just held her. We talked some more and the talking turned to kissing. Just as my night was turning around, there was a knock on the penthouse door. It was her father coming to take her home.

An hour later, my dad and I were chilling in the suite. His cell kept ringing. When he finally looked at the number, I could tell he was upset.

"Who is it?" I asked.

"Oh, it's nobody, it's nobody."

But when he didn't answer it, it rang again.

"Dad, you better get that phone. It's okay. We talked about it. You can handle the media; you can't control the weather."

My dad abruptly picked it up. "Yeah, what do you want?"

I could hear a lady's frantic voice through the phone. "I want to talk to him! I want to make sure he's okay!"

"Who wants to make sure I'm okay, Dad?" I asked.

My father covered the phone and questioned, "You can hear her?"

"Let me talk to my son!" the lady said.

I was shocked. It was my mom. Anger brewed inside. My dad had told me for years that he didn't know exactly where my mom was. Now what could he say? He had her number. She had his. I gave him a look of disgust and headed to the door to leave. He tried to stop me.

"Son, don't go. I can explain."

Feeling betrayed, I said, "What, Dad? What you got to say for yourself? You lied to me, and now that lie is completely exposed."

CHAPTER SEVEN

Worked Out

Knowing that my parents had been keeping my mom's whereabouts from me hurt worse than a punch in the gut. I wanted to get back in my car and drive home, even though it was the middle of the night and I'd just been through a dramatic experience. I sure needed to sleep. However, that was the last thing I wanted to do. I just wanted to go home and get as far away from my dad as possible. I knew he couldn't leave right away because he still had to deal with all that was going on in Savannah.

Halfway to the elevator I realized I left my keys in the suite. I had to turn around and go back to retrieve them. I bumped straight into my father.

"Move."

"We can talk about this."

"No, Dad, there's nothing to talk about. We don't need to talk about this at all. You've known where Mom was, and you haven't told me. She's known where I am, and she hasn't wanted to come see me."

"Son, it's more complicated than that. Please, Stone, please! After everything we've been through, can we just talk about this?"

But I quickly brushed past my dad, got my bag, turned out of the bedroom, snatched my keys from off the coffee table, and bolted out the door. Luckily Thorne wasn't there because my dad would've told him to stop me. There was another bodyguard posted outside my dad's door, but he wasn't getting involved with family problems even though my dad was looking at him like, *Stop my son from going anywhere.*

The elevator door would not open. I just kept pressing the button over and over like that was going to make it hurry up or something.

"It's too late for you to get on the road," my dad said as he blocked my entry onto the elevator.

"Mr. House just left."

"He's an adult. He's probably used to driving late at night. You're not, son. You haven't had an ounce of sleep yet tonight."

"I have school tomorrow, and I don't plan on missing it."

"With all you've been through, you can get an excuse for school. You don't need to go, son."

The elevator finally opened. I ducked under his arms, stepped onto it, and punched the close-door button. My dad needed to get the hint that he wasn't the boss of me. Like he'd decided to keep info about my mom to himself, I was going to do what I wanted from now on. The elevator stopped on nearly every floor. Since I'd come from the penthouse twenty-two stories up, I was irritated by the time I reached the bottom.

Wouldn't you know it, I couldn't get to my car because Thorne and some other security guys were at the entranceway. With little patience, I said to him, "I'm not going back up there."

"I'm not trying to take you back up there. I'm just trying to talk."

"I need to get on the road."

"If you insist. Your dad is going to have one of these guys drive you."

Knowing I had no choice, I gave in. "Fine. Whatever."

"Your father does care, Stone."

"I could've had my mom in my life for years. He told me he didn't know where she was. I find out that's a lie, and I'm supposed to be okay with it? The hell I am!"

"Watch your mouth," Thorne said as he grabbed my collar.

I quickly pushed his hand off of me. "When you help the devil, you don't deserve respect."

Thorne seethed. I didn't take back what I'd said. When he saw I wasn't moving, he motioned for one of the paid guards beside him to follow me.

"I'm Brandon. Can I have your keys, sir?" the guard asked.

"Are you going to be taking me home?"

"Those are my orders."

"All right," I said. I reluctantly handed over the keys to him.

And as soon as we got on the interstate

heading back toward the Atlanta area, I was out like a light.

"He's going to hate me. I'm not going to be able to tell him the truth," a female voice was saying.

"We can't lie to him—not anymore," I thought I heard my dad respond.

Was I dreaming? My dad was still in Savannah. The last thing I remembered was conking out on the couch; I'd been too tired to make it to my bed. I kept hearing voices, so I forced my eyes to open, and though the image wasn't clear, it looked like an older version of the mom I remembered in my mind. She was talking to my dad. I jumped up.

"Mom? Dad? What are y'all doing here?"

"I just want to hold you!" my mom said.

She rushed to my side, but before she could touch me, I jerked away from her. I did not want her to put one hand on me. I kept her at arm's length.

"No," I yelled like a kid throwing a tantrum.

My dad said, "Son, she's your mother."

"The mother who abandoned me."

At this, my mom plopped on the couch and started bawling. My dad looked at me like, *How could you do that to her?* I didn't feel any remorse. I didn't feel bad or guilty about wanting her to stay away. My mom seemed to understand that she had a lot to make up for. With a visible effort, she pulled herself together.

"Okay. Okay. I can do this. I live in Nashville, Stone."

"Nashville? Right up the street?" I questioned.

"Yes," she said with enthusiasm, not picking up on the fact that I was ticked.

"I thought you were in LA somewhere, Mom."

"I moved back from Hollywood about a year ago, and I contacted your father then."

Turning to my dad with a disappointed face, I said, "You've known for that long?"

"No. I didn't tell him where I was," my mom tried to explain.

Letting them know I could connect the dots, I challenged, "And he couldn't see from your phone number?"

She defended, "No. I still have an LA number.

He didn't know where I was. When I finally told him I was in Nashville, we made plans for me to come down to see you. It was supposed to be a surprise. But then I lost my nerve and didn't come. Then we tried to plan it for another day, and I did the same thing again."

My dad came close and said, "Your mom just kept repeating the pattern, and I couldn't afford to tell you that she was close because I didn't want her to break your heart again. I told her not to contact you until she was fully ready to see you and explain where she's been and why she went away."

"I have no excuse other than that I've been strung out, on and off drugs for years. Every time I got ready to see you, I relapsed. I'd get so nervous that I'd take something to try to calm down, and then I was in no condition to see anyone." She looked so sad.

Maybe I did get my name legitimately. I certainly understood how addictive drugs could be. To know how they crippled both of my parents, I realized I wasn't going to let drugs ruin my life anymore.

"I don't want you to think I'm still using,

because I'm not. I'm ready to be your mother. When I heard about the fatalities at the concert, I was so afraid you might have been one of them. So I called your dad and demanded to know if you were okay. I knew if your life was spared, I had to come and see you. Your dad told me you were angry. He left shortly after you did, and I left Nashville around the same time. We've been watching you sleep for an hour. I know it's not going to be easy to let me back in your life. But if you're willing to try, I promise I won't ever leave you again."

Filled with emotion, I hugged her as tight as I could. I was crying the same way I had as a little boy when she'd left so many years ago. But this was a different day. My mom was back, and while I wasn't sure that I could trust her not to leave again, I was starting to think that maybe things could be better.

Being in school actually wasn't that bad. Last time I was in the building I was like a pariah. No one wanted to be around me, and everyone was talking about me. Now people were talking about me, but they were coming up to me too.

Different folks were saying, "Are you okay? Is everything all right? We heard about the storm. We thought you were dead."

I really appreciated that people were concerned, but the main reason why I came to school was because I wanted to see Victoria and make sure she was all right as well. We shared a lot of intimate details and got real close. I hoped she'd enjoyed it all as much as I had. When I saw her, she was cheery and bright. She seemed surprised to see me. We hugged for a minute. I was still a little sore, but I liked her touch.

We walked to lit class together. I hadn't asked her out or anything, but I thought it was understood that I really cared. But before class began, she reminded me that she wasn't officially my girl. Then, when our teacher told the class about how we'd survived the storm and helped save other concertgoers, Victoria became overwhelmed and asked to be excused from class. I didn't see her again until the end of the day, when we bumped into each other outside of our respective locker rooms. She looked like she was doing better emotionally. My emotions, on the other hand, were starting to get the better of me.

"Okay, Stone. I can tell you're worried. What's going on? We made it through last night. We can make it through anything."

Looking at the beauty, I said, "Yeah, that's true. It's just that we have a big game coming up, and I guess I just don't want to be fake with these guys anymore."

"Is it not enough that you're planning to quit taking all that stuff?"

"Speaking of quitting bad habits, did you eat today?" We had different lunches, so I hadn't been able to see for myself.

"Yup, and I kept it all down. But don't try to change the subject. This is about you."

I looked away because I didn't have the answers. If I was a real friend and a real team-mate, could I continue lying to the guys and to my coach? Could I be true to myself if I was hold-ing something back from them?

"Well, maybe you need to talk to somebody," Victoria uttered, catching me off guard.

"I'm not crazy. I don't need to talk to some shrink."

"I'm not trying to offend you. I don't think you're crazy at all. You've just been through a

lot. Talking to someone about all you've been going through isn't a bad thing. I did it."

"Who did you talk to?"

"My coach. She's a guidance counselor here."

Not wanting to offend, I said, "Don't take this the wrong way, but I don't think I could talk to her about my problems."

"It's fine. I understand that you'd probably prefer to talk to a guy. Can you talk to your coach?"

"Yeah, but if I tell him all of what's going on, he might be forced to bench me. I'm not sure if that's what I really want, Victoria. I mean, it might be what I deserve … I don't know. I just have a lot to think about."

"Don't stress out about it. Just go with your gut. You're thinking clearly now, and I'm here if you need me."

She stood on her tiptoes and kissed my cheek. Dang, that girl had me. I wanted to scoop her up, blow the high school, and head some place where we could be together.

As soon as I stepped foot in the locker room, Ryder, Ford, Hagen, and a bunch of other guys were standing right there, happy to see

me. Then they started chanting, "Hero! Hero! Hero!"

"I'm not a hero, okay?"

"Yeah, whatever," Ryder said. "You helped some people survive a crazy accident. That makes you a hero. Coach wants to see you in his office." Ryder leaned in closer to me. "You got my text, right?"

"I did, and we need to talk."

"Is that Stone Bush?" Coach Swords called out. "The rest of you guys go on to practice."

I slowly walked to his office. The last place I wanted to be was with a man I admired. I couldn't bring myself to lie.

"I wanted to talk to you, son," he said. "Have a seat."

I complied.

"Well, I have to thank you," he smiled and said.

Confused, I asked, "Thank me?"

"Yeah, for not being able to get me any tickets. I could have been at that concert last night." He stood up and came around to sit on the front of his desk. "I'm just playing, but I'm glad you're okay."

"Yeah. I need to talk to you, Coach," I said,

ready to tell all.

"No, I don't think you do. Your dad called me this morning. He and I had a long talk. He's going to get me a signed picture so I can give it to my lady."

"What did my dad say about me?" I asked in a timid tone.

"Basically he explained to me that you haven't been thinking clearly over the past couple of weeks. He said you've been a little sick and had to take some medicine that didn't agree with your body. He said you realized it wasn't the best thing for you, and you're done with it now. All I need you to say is that you're done with that, and you're going to keep it moving."

Not wanting to be let off the hook, I said, "But, Coach, I want to—"

"Nope, I don't need you telling me any details. I just need you to tell me you're done with that."

"I am, Coach. I just hope I can play on the same level without it. You know?"

Coach leaned in, got as close to my face as he possibly could, and said, "Look. You're one of the hardest working people on this team. You and

your little crew—Hagen, Ryder, Ford, and now Emerson—all of you cats have an opportunity to be Division 1 FBS players. Don't get in your own way. Don't screw up your future by gambling on something you don't need to take a chance on. You want to bet on anything? Bet on yourself, not on pills that have a myriad of side effects. You could end up in the ground from messing with some of that stuff. You know?"

"Yes, sir, Coach," I said, truly appreciating his talk.

"I hear your mom's back in your life too."

"My dad's got a big mouth. What else did he tell you?"

"He told me he's proud of you. He loves you, and he plans to be at Friday's game."

"He said all that?" I said, shocked and amazed. "He really said that?"

Coach confirmed it. I gave him dap. Then he dismissed me to go to practice.

When I jogged onto the field, I saw my crew. Back in the summer, Ford, Ryder, Hagen, and I had all worked out together, and now Emerson was stretching with them too. I joined in. After a few moments, I decided to just come out with it.

"I don't want to be fake with you guys, so I have to tell y'all something. I've been on steroids."

"Tell us something we don't know," Ryder said, as if the news didn't faze him.

"Yeah, man. We all do stupid stuff sometimes. I'm glad you want to come clean to us and all, but we're just glad you're alive and that you've come to your senses and realized you don't need that stuff anymore," Emerson said. He playfully knocked me on the shoulder.

"We all got things we're running from," Hagen said as he looked at me in a way that made me a little nervous for him. "But friendship can get us through anything, right?"

All five of us nodded.

"And you don't need to go confessing to nobody else. We got your back. But if you use that stuff again and don't share, I'm gonna kill you," Ryder teased. We all laughed.

For the first time in a long time, I felt the solidarity between all of us. My boys cared. I felt really good.

During the game, I had dropped every pass that was thrown to me. To make matters

worse, Coach had pulled me and put in Jaboe, the tight end who had been chasing my butt since we started the season. He'd caught all his passes. I was being a poor sportsman about it too. I couldn't even be happy for someone who'd watched me run up and down the field all year.

After the game I got on the football players' bus because I didn't want to hang out with all the couples on the co-ed bus. But then I decided I wanted to see Victoria, so I went to sit with her on the other bus. However, I couldn't shake my bad mood, and I ended up snapping at her and getting back on the football players' bus. Man, I just didn't feel like hearing somebody say something positive when I felt like crap.

Back on the players' bus, Hagen sat beside me. He couldn't take a hint that I wanted to ride solo all the way back to Grovehill. So I had to slide over.

"I ain't trying to talk, man," I said to him.

"Cool, then just listen. You got skills, Stone. You might think you need something extra to make the plays you've been making all year. I'm not naive, so I'm not going to sit here and say you didn't have an edge when you were on those

pills. But what I am trying to tell you is we all have bad games. Shake it off and get ready to fight another day. You just lived through a crazy storm, and I live in a neighborhood where shots are fired all the time. Those are real problems."

He was right. He was absolutely telling the truth. Here I was having a pity party because I hadn't gotten a touchdown, grabbed a great catch, or been the man in the game, all because I was feeling like I didn't have enough on the inside to play hard. Really I wasn't even going all out because, mentally, I just felt like I couldn't do it. I was getting in my own way, and I had to learn to chill.

"Thanks, man," I said as I jabbed him in the arm.

When we got to the school, I found Victoria. She wasn't interested in talking to me at first. I had to bust out my puppy dog eyes, grovel a bit, and apologize a lot to get her to hang out with me. When she finally agreed, I took her to Waffle House.

When I got home later that evening, I couldn't believe my dad was waiting up for me. He, Bishop, and Thorne had come to my game.

Wanting to impress them was probably another thing that had me down earlier.

"I usually play better than that," I said to him.

"I was just happy to see you play. No worries. You'll get them next time."

"I just don't know if I can do it, Dad. You know?"

"Of course I know. I know what it's like to want that edge that only drugs can give. But it's also destructive."

"Thanks, Dad. I really appreciate your support."

"I should've been there for you all along, son. But from now on I'll do better."

"You did have one move," Bishop said as he came out of the kitchen. "That was sweet! It looked like how I used to do it when I was in high school."

"What do you mean how you used to do it?" I asked.

Bishop explained, "How I used to play football when I was a wide receiver."

"Wow, I never knew that," I said.

"If I had your height and build, I probably could have gotten a scholarship. Your dad is

right. You don't need anything extra to help you take care of business on the field. You got it."

I couldn't believe that Bishop and I were seeing eye-to-eye. We'd been adversaries for so long. As devastating as that storm was, it changed us for the better. I headed on up to go to bed, until I heard footsteps behind me. Quickly I turned and saw Thorne shaking a bottle of pills.

"If you want these, they're yours," Thorne said.

I couldn't believe he was tempting me. Up till now he'd only rationed me a few steroid pills here and there. Now he was practically giving me a whole bottle.

"What?" I said. "No thank you."

"You sure? You good?"

"I mean, I know my game was wack today, but I just gotta understand my body and trust it to do more than my mind limits it to do, you know? I don't need that. Thanks."

"Oh, I see how it is!"

And we wrestled, hitting the walls in the hallway. Bishop and my dad ran to see what we were doing. My dad was cheering for me to pin Thorne, and Bishop was too. It was like they got in my head, or Thorne felt bad for me and let

me win. Either way, it pumped up my ego. The four of us bachelors had a camaraderie that was special.

"Seriously, Lars," Bishop said. "What are you gonna do now that Heather is gone?"

"I know, right? I got to find somebody. We really need to do damage control with this storm. I need to find a president who's not going to be gloomy. I don't need someone who's going to want me."

"Yeah, for sure. You definitely don't need somebody whose whole world revolves around you. You need a married lady," Thorne added.

"Wait. I know somebody!" I said to my dad.

"Who do you know?" Bishop said.

I flicked Bishop off with my hand and said, "No, I'm serious. Dad, you talked to her."

"Who?" my dad questioned.

"Victoria's mom!" When he seemed unsure, I added, "She's married. She's got a family. She's a big fan of yours. She knows a lot about Sweet Lips, and she needs a job."

He shook his head. "All right, all right. Well, I got to meet her."

"Yeah, you need to meet her because we got

to get stuff fixed up for the tour," Bishop said.

When I went in my room, there was a note from my mom. I opened it up. It read:

> Dear Stone,
>
> Thank you for hearing me out the other day. Boy, have I missed you, and I am so proud of the man you've grown into. You know you're a better person than me and your father. I was sincere when I said I want to figure out a way to work on our relationship. I would love for you to come up and hang out with me and my husband soon—if your dad agrees and you're comfortable with that. Let's plan it.
>
> Thanksgiving and Christmas are right around the corner. Either of those times would be awesome to have you here. I can't imagine how much damage I've done to your life by not being there. Every boy should have his mom in his life to care for him and love him all the time, and for you not having that, I am sorry. I love you, Stone.
>
> Hugs,
> Mom

I held the letter close to my heart. My mom was back in my life, and for that I was so grateful.

My dad was serious about asking Victoria's mom to be the president of his fan club and in charge of his foundation. She was pretty shocked at the offer, but she graciously accepted.

We got invited to Victoria's father's birthday party later that day. After all that I'd put his daughter through, I figured I was the last person Mr. House would want to see there. But Victoria insisted, so I went. I actually liked watching her work the crowd. She was so lovely and confident. We were good for one another. We were determined not to let the other one fail or fall back into bad habits.

Knowing that she was great for me, I did the only thing I could, and that was ask her to be my girl. If I would have known how many people around us were going to say "ooh" and "ahh," I probably would have chosen a more private setting. But I stood my ground, didn't waver, and waited for her response. When she said she'd go out with me, I spun her around. Both of us had been through the mud, but now it was like we

had a fresh opportunity to start over and not fall.

Victoria learned her body was perfect the way it was, and I learned the same. Coach and my friends knew I had issues, but they weren't against me. They were on my side. I was not going to let them down ever again. Now I had to stand firm and believe in me. Finally my life was good, and for now, all the issues had been worked out.

STEPHANIE PERRY MOORE is the author of many YA inspirational fiction titles, including the *Lockwood Lions* series, the *Payton Skky* series, the *Laurel Shadrach* series, the *Perry Skky Jr.* series, the *Yasmin Peace* series, the *Faith Thomas Novelzine* series, the *Carmen Browne* series, the *Morgan Love* series, and the *Beta Gamma Pi* series. Mrs. Moore speaks with young people across the country, encouraging them to achieve every attainable dream. She currently lives in the greater Atlanta area with her husband, Derrick, and their three children. Visit her website at www. stephanieperrymoore.com.

DERRICK MOORE is a former NFL running back and currently the developmental coach for the Georgia Institute of Technology. He is also the author of *The Great Adventure* and *It's Possible: Turning Your Dreams into Reality*. Mr. Moore is a motivational speaker and shares with audiences everywhere how to climb the mountain in their lives and not stop until they have reached the top. He and his wife, Stephanie, have co-authored the *Alec London* series. Visit his website at www.derrickmoorespeaking.com.

WANT A DIFFERENT
point of view?

JUST *flip* THE BOOK!